This Christmas Planner
Belongs To

____

Date __________________

For more information about Scott & Rebecca M. Norris, access their websites (www.scott-norris.com) or (www.rebeccanorrisbooks.com).

Hardcover ISBN: 979-8-9850971-7-7
Paperback ISBN: 979-8-9850971-6-0

Library of Congress Control Number: 2022910769

Edited by Scott Norris & Rebecca M. Norris
Cover art by Jill Wellington via Pixabay under Pixabay License (www.pixabay.com) with additions by Rebecca M. Norris, used by permission
Layout by Rebecca M. Norris

Printed by Duskraven Entertainment, LLC in the USA.

Duskraven Entertainment, LLC
PO Box 3795
Olathe KS 66063

www.rebeccanorrisbooks.com

Activities Planner

Generously

By Scott Norris

One gift was all
A gesture small
For Joy did call
To feelings small

Christmas is near,
My dread and fear,
I lost those dear,
No friends come near.

You gave to me,
Generously
Joking were we
Laughing freely

A gift it's true
To me from you
Small acts can do,
More than I knew

Thank you once more
Joy is here for,
Myself once more,
Hope holds my core.

Merry Christmas!

DECEMBER 01

Today's Activities:

☐ ______________________   ☐ ______________________
☐ ______________________   ☐ ______________________
☐ ______________________   ☐ ______________________
☐ ______________________   ☐ ______________________
☐ ______________________   ☐ ______________________

Things To Remember:

☐ ______________________   ☐ ______________________
☐ ______________________   ☐ ______________________
☐ ______________________   ☐ ______________________
☐ ______________________   ☐ ______________________
☐ ______________________   ☐ ______________________
☐ ______________________   ☐ ______________________

Christmas Song of the Day!

"Joy to the World" Isaac Watts

Joy to the world! the Lord is come;
Let Earth receive her King;
Let every heart prepare him room,
And heaven and nature sing,
And heaven and nature sing,
And heaven, and heaven, and nature sing.

No more let sins and sorrows grow,
Nor thorns infest the ground;
He comes to make His blessings flow
Far as the curse is found,
Far as the curse is found,
Far as, far as, the curse is found.

Joy to the world! the Savior reigns;
Let men their songs employ;
While fields and floods, rocks, hills, and plains
Repeat the sounding joy,
Repeat the sounding joy,
Repeat, repeat the sounding joy.

He rules the world with truth and grace,
And makes the nations prove
The glories of His righteousness,
And wonders of His love,
And wonders of His love,
And wonders, wonders, of His love.

The practice of baking and eating Gingerbread Houses was inspired by the fairytale *Hansel & Gretel!*

DECEMBER 02

Today's Activities:

Things To Remember:

Christmas Song of the Day!
"I Heard the Bells on Christmas Day" Henry Wadsworth Longfellow

I heard the bells on Christmas Day
Their old, familiar carols play,
and wild and sweet
The words repeat
Of peace on earth, good-will to men!

And thought how, as the day had come,
The belfries of all Christendom
Had rolled along
The unbroken song
Of peace on earth, good-will to men!

Till ringing, singing on its way,
The world revolved from night to day,
A voice, a chime,
A chant sublime
Of peace on earth, good-will to men!

Then from each black, accursed mouth
The cannon thundered in the South,
And with the sound

The carols drowned
Of peace on earth, good-will to men!

It was as if an earthquake rent
The hearth-stones of a continent,
And made forlorn
The households born
Of peace on earth, good-will to men!

And in despair I bowed my head;
"There is no peace on earth," I said;
"For hate is strong,
And mocks the song
Of peace on earth, good-will to men!"

Then pealed the bells more loud and deep:
"God is not dead, nor doth He sleep;
The Wrong shall fail,
The Right prevail,
With peace on earth, good-will to men."

Which country started the tradition of putting up a Christmas tree?

Germany

DECEMBER 03

Today's Activities:

- [ ] _______________
- [ ] _______________
- [ ] _______________
- [ ] _______________
- [ ] _______________

- [ ] _______________
- [ ] _______________
- [ ] _______________
- [ ] _______________
- [ ] _______________

Things To Remember:

- [ ] _______________
- [ ] _______________
- [ ] _______________
- [ ] _______________
- [ ] _______________

- [ ] _______________
- [ ] _______________
- [ ] _______________
- [ ] _______________
- [ ] _______________

Christmas Song of the Day!
"O Come All Ye Faithful" John Francis Wade

O come, all ye faithful, joyful and triumphant!
O come ye, O come ye to Bethlehem;
Come and behold him
Born the King of Angels:
O come, let us adore Him, (3×)
Christ the Lord

God of God, light of light,
Lo, he abhors not the Virgin's womb;
Very God, begotten, not created:
O come, let us adore Him, (3×)
Christ the Lord.

Sing, choirs of angels, sing in exultation,
Sing, all ye citizens of Heaven above!
Glory to God, glory in the highest:
O come, let us adore Him, (3×)
Christ the Lord.

Yea, Lord, we greet thee, born this happy morning;
Jesus, to thee be glory given!
Word of the Father, now in flesh appearing!
O come, let us adore Him, (3×)
Christ the Lord.

What is the best-selling Christmas song ever?
"White Christmas" by Bing Crosby

DECEMBER 04

Today's Activities:

Things To Remember:

Christmas Song of the Day!

"Jingle Bells" James Lord Pierpont

Dashing through the snow
In a one-horse open sleigh
O'er the fields we go
Laughing all the way

Bells on bob tail ring
Making spirits bright
What fun it is to ride and sing
A sleighing song tonight!

Jingle bells, jingle bells,
Jingle all the way.
Oh! what fun it is to ride
In a one-horse open sleigh.

Jingle bells, jingle bells,
Jingle all the way;
Oh! what fun it is to ride
In a one-horse open sleigh.

A day or two ago
I thought I'd take a ride
And soon, Miss Fanny Bright
Was seated by my side,
The horse was lean and lank
Misfortune seemed his lot
He got into a drifted bank
And then we got upsot.
|: chorus :|

A day or two ago,
The story I must tell
I went out on the snow,
And on my back I fell;
A gent was riding by
In a one-horse open sleigh,
He laughed as there I sprawling lie,
But quickly drove away.
|: chorus :|

Now the ground is white
Go it while you're young,
Take the girls tonight
and sing this sleighing song;
Just get a bobtailed bay
Two forty as his speed
Hitch him to an open sleigh
And crack! you'll take the lead.
|: chorus :|

What popular Christmas song was actually written for Thanksgiving?

"Jingle Bells"

DECEMBER 05

Today's Activities:

- ☐ ______________________   ☐ ______________________
- ☐ ______________________   ☐ ______________________
- ☐ ______________________   ☐ ______________________
- ☐ ______________________   ☐ ______________________
- ☐ ______________________   ☐ ______________________

Things To Remember:

- ☐ ______________________   ☐ ______________________
- ☐ ______________________   ☐ ______________________
- ☐ ______________________   ☐ ______________________
- ☐ ______________________   ☐ ______________________
- ☐ ______________________   ☐ ______________________
- ☐ ______________________   ☐ ______________________

Christmas Song of the Day!

"Angels We Have Heard On High" James Chadwick

Angels we have heard on high
Sweetly singing o'er the plains
And the mountains in reply
Echoing their joyous strains
Gloria in excelsis Deo!
Gloria in excelsis Deo!

Come to Bethlehem and see
Him whose birth the angels sing;
Come, adore on bended knee,
Christ the Lord, the newborn King.
Gloria in excelsis Deo!
Gloria in excelsis Deo!

Shepherds, why this jubilee?
Why your joyous strains prolong?
What the gladsome tidings be?
Which inspire your heavenly songs?
Gloria in excelsis Deo!
Gloria in excelsis Deo!

Rudolph The Red-Nosed Reindeer started off as a marketing gimmick for Montgomery Ward!

DECEMBER 06

Today's Activities:

- ☐ __________________
- ☐ __________________
- ☐ __________________
- ☐ __________________
- ☐ __________________

- ☐ __________________
- ☐ __________________
- ☐ __________________
- ☐ __________________
- ☐ __________________

Things To Remember:

- ☐ __________________
- ☐ __________________
- ☐ __________________
- ☐ __________________
- ☐ __________________
- ☐ __________________

- ☐ __________________
- ☐ __________________
- ☐ __________________
- ☐ __________________
- ☐ __________________
- ☐ __________________

Christmas Song of the Day!

"Good King Wenceslas" John Mason Neale

Good King Wences'las looked out,
on the Feast of Stephen,
When the snow lay round about,
deep and crisp and even;
Brightly shone the moon that night,
tho' the frost was cruel,
When a poor man came in sight,
gath'ring winter fuel.

"Hither, page, and stand by me,
if thou know'st it, telling,
Yonder peasant, who is he?
Where and what his dwelling?"
"Sire, he lives a good league hence,
underneath the mountain;

Right against the forest fence,
by Saint Agnes' fountain."

"Bring me flesh, and bring me wine,
bring me pine logs hither:
Thou and I shall see him dine,
when we bear them thither."

Page and monarch, forth they went,
forth they went together;
Through the rude wind's wild lament
and the bitter weather.

"Sire, the night is darker now,
and the wind blows stronger;
Fails my heart, I know not how;
I can go no longer."

"Mark my footsteps, good my page.
Tread thou in them boldly
Thou shalt find the winter's rage
freeze thy blood less coldly."

In his master's steps he trod,
where the snow lay dinted;
Heat was in the very sod
which the saint had printed.
Therefore, Christian men, be sure,
wealth or rank possessing,
Ye who now will bless the poor,
shall yourselves find blessing.

As the clock chimes midnight to ring in the New Year, a Spanish tradition involves eating twelve grapes — one for each chime!

DECEMBER 07

Today's Activities:

- ☐ __________________
- ☐ __________________
- ☐ __________________
- ☐ __________________
- ☐ __________________

- ☐ __________________
- ☐ __________________
- ☐ __________________
- ☐ __________________
- ☐ __________________

Things To Remember:

- ☐ __________________
- ☐ __________________
- ☐ __________________
- ☐ __________________
- ☐ __________________

- ☐ __________________
- ☐ __________________
- ☐ __________________
- ☐ __________________
- ☐ __________________

Christmas Song of the Day!

"In The Bleak Midwinter" Christina Rossetti

In the bleak mid-winter
Frosty wind made moan;
Earth stood hard as iron,
Water like a stone;
Snow had fallen, snow on snow,
Snow on snow,
In the bleak mid-winter
Long ago.

When He comes to reign:
In the bleak mid-winter
A stable-place sufficed
The Lord God Almighty —
Jesus Christ.

Our God, heaven cannot hold Him
Nor earth sustain,
Heaven and earth shall flee away

Enough for Him, whom cherubim
Worship night and day,
A breastful of milk
And a mangerful of hay;
Enough for Him, whom Angels
Fall down before,
The ox and ass and camel
Which adore.

Angels and Archangels
May have gathered there,
Cherubim and seraphim

Thronged the air;
But only His Mother
In her maiden bliss
Worshipped the
Beloved
With a kiss.

What can I give Him,
Poor as I am? —
If I were a Shepherd
I would bring a lamb;
If I were a Wise Man
I would do my part, —
Yet what I can I give
Him, —
Give my heart.

What's the most popular kind of tree to use for a Christmas tree?

A Nordmann Fir

DECEMBER 08

Today's Activities:

Things To Remember:

Christmas Song of the Day!
"I Saw Three Ships" Unknown

I saw three ships come sailing in
On Christmas Day, on Christmas Day;
I saw three ships come sailing in
On Christmas Day in the morning.

And who was in those ships all three,
On Christmas Day, on Christmas Day?
And whp was in those ships all three,
On Christmas Day in the morning?

Our Saviour Christ and his ladye,
On Christmas Day, on Christmas Day;
Our Saviour Christ and his ladye,
On Christmas Day in the morning.

Pray whither sailed those ships all three,
On Christmas Day, on Christmas Day?
Pray whither sailed those ships all three,
On Christmas Day in the morning?

O they sailed into Bethlehem,
On Christmas Day, on Christmas Day;
O they sailed into Bethlehem,
On Christmas Day in the morning.

And all the bells on Earth shall ring,
On Christmas Day, on Christmas Day;
And all the bells on Earth shall ring,
On Christmas Day in the morning.

And all the angels in Heaven shall sing,
On Christmas Day, on Christmas Day;
And all the angels in Heaven shall sing,
On Christmas Day in the morning.

And all the souls on Earth shall sing,
On Christmas Day, on Christmas Day;
And all the souls on Earth shall sing,
On Christmas Day in the morning.

How many ghosts are there in 'A Christmas Carol?' Four

DECEMBER 09

Today's Activities:

- ☐ __________________
- ☐ __________________
- ☐ __________________
- ☐ __________________
- ☐ __________________

- ☐ __________________
- ☐ __________________
- ☐ __________________
- ☐ __________________
- ☐ __________________

Things To Remember:

- ☐ __________________
- ☐ __________________
- ☐ __________________
- ☐ __________________
- ☐ __________________
- ☐ __________________

- ☐ __________________
- ☐ __________________
- ☐ __________________
- ☐ __________________
- ☐ __________________
- ☐ __________________

Christmas Song of the Day!
"Oh Little Town of Bethlehem" Phillips Brooks

O little town of Bethlehem,
How still we see thee lie!
Above thy deep and dreamless sleep
The silent stars go by.
Yet in thy dark streets shineth
The everlasting Light;
The hopes and fears of all the years
Are met in thee to-night.

O morning stars, together
Proclaim the holy birth!
And praises sing to God the King,
And peace to men on earth.
For Christ is born of Mary
And gathered all above,
While mortals sleep the Angels keep
Their watch of wondering love.

How silently, how silently,
The wondrous gift is given;
So God imparts to human hearts
The blessings of His Heaven.
No ear may hear His coming,
But in this world of sin,
Where meek souls will receive Him still,
The dear Christ enters in.

Where children pure and happy
Pray to the blessed Child,
Where misery cries out to Thee,
Son of the Mother mild;1

Where Charity stands watching
And Faith holds wide the door,
The dark night wakes, the glory breaks,
And Christmas comes once more.

O holy Child of Bethlehem,
Descend to us, we pray!
Cast out our sin and enter in,
Be born in us to-day.
We hear the Christmas angels,
The great glad tidings tell;
O come to us, abide with us,
Our Lord Emmanuel!

Who helped Rudolph after he left the North Pole?
Hermey the Elf and Yukon Cornelius

DECEMBER 10

Today's Activities:

- [ ] __________________
- [ ] __________________
- [ ] __________________
- [ ] __________________
- [ ] __________________

- [ ] __________________
- [ ] __________________
- [ ] __________________
- [ ] __________________
- [ ] __________________

Things To Remember:

- [ ] __________________
- [ ] __________________
- [ ] __________________
- [ ] __________________
- [ ] __________________
- [ ] __________________

- [ ] __________________
- [ ] __________________
- [ ] __________________
- [ ] __________________
- [ ] __________________
- [ ] __________________

Christmas Song of the Day!
"Go Tell It On The Mountain" John Wesley Work Jr.

While shepherds kept their watching
O'er silent flocks by night,
Behold throughout the heavens
There shone a holy light

Chorus:
Go, tell it on the mountain
Over the hills and everywhere
Go, tell it on the mountain
That Jesus Christ is born.

The shepherds feared and trembled
When lo! above the earth
Rang out the angel chorus
That hailed our Saviour's birth;

Chorus

Down in a lowly manger
The humble Christ was born;
And God sent out salvation
That blessed Christmas morn.

Chorus

When I was a seeker
I sought both night and day
I sought the Lord to help me
And He showed me the way.

Chorus

He made me a watchman
Upon the city wall
And If I am a Christian
I am the least of all.

Chorus

Dried out Christmas trees spark roughly 100 accidental fires each holiday season!

DECEMBER 11

Today's Activities:

Things To Remember:

Christmas Song of the Day!
"God Rest Ye Merry Gentleman" Unknown

God rest you merry, gentlemen,
Let nothing you dismay,
For Jesus Christ our Savior
Was born upon this day,
To save us all from Satan's power
When we were gone astray:
O tidings of comfort and joy,
comfort and joy,
O tidings of comfort and joy.

From God our heavenly Father
A blessed angel came,
And unto certain shepherds
Brought tidings of the same,
The shepherds at those tidings
Rejoiced much in mind,
And left their flocks a-feeding
In tempest, storm and wind,
And went to Bethlehem
straightway,
This blessed Babe to find:
O tidings of comfort and joy,
comfort and joy,
O tidings of comfort and joy.

But when to Bethlehem they
came,
Whereat this Infant lay,
They found Him in a manger,
Where oxen feed on hay;
His mother Mary kneeling,
Unto the Lord did pray:
O tidings of comfort and joy,
comfort and joy,
O tidings of comfort and joy.

Now to the Lord sing praises,
All you within this place,
And with true love and
brotherhood
Each other now embrace;
This holy tide of Christmas
All other doth deface:
O tidings of comfort and joy,
comfort and joy,
O tidings of comfort and joy.

Using evergreens to mark the winter solstice is a tradition dating back to the ancient Egyptians!

DECEMBER 12

Today's Activities:

Things To Remember:

Christmas Song of the Day!
"We Wish You A Merry Christmas" Unknown

We wish you a merry Christmas
We wish you a merry Christmas
We wish you a merry Christmas and a happy new year
Good tidings we bring to you and your kin
We wish you a merry Christmas and a happy new year

Oh, bring us some figgy pudding
Oh, bring us some figgy pudding
Oh, bring us some figgy pudding
And bring it right here

Good tidings we bring to you and your kin
We wish you a merry Christmas and a happy new year
We won't go until we get some
We won't go until we get some

We won't go until we get some
So bring it right here

Good tidings we bring to you and your kin
We wish you a merry Christmas and a happy new year
We all like our figgy pudding
We all like our figgy pudding
We all like our figgy pudding
With all its good cheers

Good tidings we bring to you and your kin
We wish you a merry Christmas and a happy new year
We wish you a merry Christmas
We wish you a merry Christmas
We wish you a merry Christmas and a happy new year

How long does it take for a tree to reach average,
ideal "Christmas tree" height?

15 years

DECEMBER 13

Today's Activities:

- [ ] ______________________
- [ ] ______________________
- [ ] ______________________
- [ ] ______________________
- [ ] ______________________

- [ ] ______________________
- [ ] ______________________
- [ ] ______________________
- [ ] ______________________
- [ ] ______________________

Things To Remember:

- [ ] ______________________
- [ ] ______________________
- [ ] ______________________
- [ ] ______________________
- [ ] ______________________
- [ ] ______________________

- [ ] ______________________
- [ ] ______________________
- [ ] ______________________
- [ ] ______________________
- [ ] ______________________
- [ ] ______________________

Christmas Song of the Day!
"O Come O Come Emmanuel" Translated by John Mason Neale

O come, O come, Emmanuel,
And ransom captive Israel,
That mourns in lonely exile here,
Until the Son of God appear.
Rejoice! Rejoice! Emmanuel
Shall come to thee, O Israel.

O come, Thou Rod of Jesse, free
Thine own from Satan's tyranny;
From depths of hell Thy people save,
And give them victory o'er the grave.
Rejoice! Rejoice! Emmanuel
Shall come to thee, O Israel.

O come, Thou Dayspring, from on high,
And cheer us by Thy drawing nigh;
Disperse the gloomy clouds of night,
And death's dark shadows put to flight.
Rejoice! Rejoice! Emmanuel
Shall come to thee, O Israel.

O come, Thou Key of David, come
And open wide our heav'nly home;
Make safe the way that leads on high,
And close the path to misery.
Rejoice! Rejoice! Emmanuel
Shall come to thee, O Israel.

O come, Adonai, Lord of might,
Who to Thy tribes, on Sinai's height,
In ancient times didst give the law
In cloud and majesty and awe.
Rejoice! Rejoice! Emmanuel
Shall come to thee, O Israel.

How do you say Merry Christmas in Hawaiian?
Mele Kalikimaka

DECEMBER 14

Today's Activities:

- ☐ ___________________
- ☐ ___________________
- ☐ ___________________
- ☐ ___________________
- ☐ ___________________

- ☐ ___________________
- ☐ ___________________
- ☐ ___________________
- ☐ ___________________
- ☐ ___________________

Things To Remember:

- ☐ ___________________
- ☐ ___________________
- ☐ ___________________
- ☐ ___________________
- ☐ ___________________

- ☐ ___________________
- ☐ ___________________
- ☐ ___________________
- ☐ ___________________
- ☐ ___________________

Christmas Song of the Day!

"For Unto Us A Child Is Born" George Frideric Handel

For unto us a Child is born, unto us a
Son is given, and the government shall
be upon His shoulder; and his name
shall be called Wonderful Counsellor,
the Mighty God, the Everlasting Father,
the Prince of Peace
(Isaiah 9:5)

According to legend, what holiday goodies were shaped to
resemble a shepherd's staff, as a way to remind children of
the shepherds who visited baby Jesus?
Candy canes

DECEMBER 15

Today's Activities:

- ☐ ___________________________
- ☐ ___________________________
- ☐ ___________________________
- ☐ ___________________________
- ☐ ___________________________

- ☐ ___________________________
- ☐ ___________________________
- ☐ ___________________________
- ☐ ___________________________
- ☐ ___________________________

Things To Remember:

- ☐ ___________________________
- ☐ ___________________________
- ☐ ___________________________
- ☐ ___________________________
- ☐ ___________________________
- ☐ ___________________________

- ☐ ___________________________
- ☐ ___________________________
- ☐ ___________________________
- ☐ ___________________________
- ☐ ___________________________
- ☐ ___________________________

Christmas Song of the Day!
"Hallelujah Chorus" George Frideric Handel

Hallelujah hallelujah hallelujah hallelujah hallelujah
Hallelujah hallelujah hallelujah hallelujah hallelujah
For lord our God omnipotent reigneth
Hallelujah hallelujah hallelujah hallelujah
For lord our God omnipotent reigneth
Hallelujah hallelujah hallelujah hallelujah
For lord our God omnipotent reigneth
Hallelujah hallelujah hallelujah hallelujah
Hallelujah hallelujah hallelujah hallelujah
Hallelujah hallelujah hallelujah hallelujah
(For the lord God omnipotent reigneth)
Hallelujah hallelujah hallelujah hallelujah
For the lord God omnipotent reigneth
(Hallelujah hallelujah hallelujah hallelujah)
Hallelujah
The kingdom of this world;
Is become

The kingdom of our Lord,
And of His Christ
And of His Christ
And He shall reign for ever and ever
And he shall reign forever and ever
And he shall reign forever and ever
And he shall reign forever and ever
King of kings forever and ever hallelujah hallelujah
And lord of lords forever and ever hallelujah hallelujah
King of kings forever and ever hallelujah hallelujah
And lord of lords forever and ever hallelujah hallelujah

King of kings forever and ever hallelujah hallelujah
And lord of lords
King of kings and lord of lords

And he shall reign
And he shall reign
And he shall reign
He shall reign
And he shall reign forever and ever
King of kings forever and ever
And lord of lords hallelujah hallelujah
And he shall reign forever and ever
King of kings and lord of lords
King of kings and lord of lords
And he shall reign forever and ever
Forever and ever and ever and ever
(King of kings and lord of lords)
Hallelujah hallelujah hallelujah hallelujah
Hallelujah

Which U.S. state was the first to declare Christmas an official holiday? Oklahoma.

DECEMBER 16

Today's Activities:

Things To Remember:

Christmas Song of the Day!
"Once In Royal David's City" Cecil Frances Alexander

Once in royal David's city
Stood a lowly cattle shed,
Where a mother laid her baby
In a manger for his bed:
Mary was that Mother mild,
Jesus Christ her little Child.

He came down to earth from
heaven
Who is God and Lord of all,
And his shelter was a stable,
And his cradle was a stall:
With the poor and mean and
lowly,
Lived on earth our Savior
holy.

And through all his
wondrous childhood
Day by day like us he
grew,
He was little, weak,
and helpless,
Tears and smiles like
us he knew:
And he feeleth for
our sadness,
And he shareth in
our gladness.

And our eyes at last shall see him
Through his own redeeming
love,
For that Child so dear and gentle,
Is our Lord in heaven above:
And he leads his children on
To the place where he is gone.

Not in that poor lowly stable,
With the oxen standing by,
We shall we see him: but in
heaven,
Set at God's right hand on high,
Where like stars his children
crowned,
All in white shall wait around.

How much do Americans spend on holiday shopping?
Americans spend an average of $942 per person on holiday
gifts.

DECEMBER 17

Today's Activities:

☐ _______________________ ☐ _______________________
☐ _______________________ ☐ _______________________
☐ _______________________ ☐ _______________________
☐ _______________________ ☐ _______________________
☐ _______________________ ☐ _______________________

Things To Remember:

☐ _______________________ ☐ _______________________
☐ _______________________ ☐ _______________________
☐ _______________________ ☐ _______________________
☐ _______________________ ☐ _______________________
☐ _______________________ ☐ _______________________
☐ _______________________ ☐ _______________________

Christmas Song of the Day!

"Away In A Manger" Martin Luther (disputed)

Away in a manger, no crib for a bed,
The little Lord Jesus laid down his sweet head.
The stars in the bright sky looked down where he lay,
The little Lord Jesus asleep on the hay.

The cattle are lowing, the baby awakes,
But little Lord Jesus, no crying he makes.
I love thee, Lord Jesus! look down from the sky,
And stay by my cradle till morning is nigh.

Be near me, Lord Jesus; I ask thee to stay
Close by me forever, and love me I pray.
Bless all the dear children in thy tender care,
And take us to heaven to live with thee there.

The Yule Log is a popular cake symbolizing the log you should burn on Christmas Eve. If the log goes out before the morning, it is believed you will face bad luck in the New Year.

DECEMBER 18

Today's Activities:

Things To Remember:

Christmas Song of the Day!

"Hark! The Herald Angels Sing" Charles Wesley & George Whitefield

Hark! The herald-angels sing
"Glory to the newborn king;
Peace on earth and mercy mild,
God and sinners reconciled"
Joyful all ye nations rise,
Join the triumph of the skies
With the angelic host proclaim
"Christ is born in Bethlehem"
Hark! The herald-angels sing
"Glory to the new-born king"

Christ, by highest heaven adored
Christ, the everlasting Lord,
Late in time behold Him come
Offspring of a Virgin's womb:
Veiled in flesh the Godhead see,
Hail the incarnate Deity
Pleased as man with man to dwell
Jesus, our Emmanuel
Hark! The herald-angels sing
"Glory to the newborn King"

Hail the Heaven-born
Prince of Peace!
Hail the Sun of Righteousness!
Light and life to all He brings,
Risen with healing in His wings;
Mild He lays His glory by
Born that man no more may die
Born to raise the sons of earth
Born to give them second birth
Hark! The herald angels sing
"Glory to the new-born king"

Prince Albert in the 1840s popularized the glitter and beauty of a Christmas tree. A prince of German descent, he introduced the concept of the Christmas tree to his young wife Queen Victoria of England. The concept became popular nearly overnight.

DECEMBER 19

Today's Activities:

- ☐ ______________________
- ☐ ______________________
- ☐ ______________________
- ☐ ______________________
- ☐ ______________________

- ☐ ______________________
- ☐ ______________________
- ☐ ______________________
- ☐ ______________________
- ☐ ______________________

Things To Remember:

- ☐ ______________________
- ☐ ______________________
- ☐ ______________________
- ☐ ______________________
- ☐ ______________________
- ☐ ______________________

- ☐ ______________________
- ☐ ______________________
- ☐ ______________________
- ☐ ______________________
- ☐ ______________________
- ☐ ______________________

Christmas Song of the Day!

"It Came Upon The Midnight Clear" Edmund Sears

It came upon the midnight clear,
That glorious song of old,
From angels bending near the earth,
To touch their harps of gold:
"Peace on the earth, goodwill to men,
From heaven's all-gracious King."
The world in solemn stillness lay,
To hear the angels sing.

Still through the cloven skies they come,
With peaceful wings unfurled,
And still their heavenly music floats
O'er all the weary world;
Above its sad and lowly plains,
They bend on hovering wing,
And ever o'er its babel sounds
The blessed angels sing.

Yet with the woes of sin and strife
The world has suffered long;
Beneath the angel-strain have rolled
Two thousand years of wrong;
And man, at war with man, hears not
The love-song which they bring;
O hush the noise, ye men of strife,
And hear the angels sing.
And ye, beneath life's crushing load,
Whose forms are bending low,
Who toil along the climbing way
With painful steps and slow,
Look now! for glad and golden hours
come swiftly on the wing.
O rest beside the weary road,
And hear the angels sing!

For lo!, the days are hastening on,
By prophet bards foretold,
When with the ever-circling years
Comes round the age of gold
When peace shall over all the earth
Its ancient splendors fling,
And the whole world give back the song
Which now the angels sing.

When gold was dropped down the chimney of the home of three poor sisters in order to help them fulfill their dowry, it created what Christmas tradition?
Stockings by the fireplace!

DECEMBER 20

Today's Activities:

Things To Remember:

Christmas Song of the Day!
"The First Noël" Unknown

The first Noël the angel did say
Was to certain poor shepherds in
fields as they lay;
In fields where they lay, keeping their
sheep,
On a cold winter's night that was so
deep:
Noël, Noël, Noël, Noël,
Born is the King of Israel.

They looked up and saw a star,
Shining in the east, beyond them far:
And to the earth it gave great light,
And so it continued both day and
night:
Noël, Noël, Noël, Noël,
Born is the King of Israel.

And by the light of that same star,
Three Wise Men came from
country far;
To seek for a King was their intent,
And to follow the star whersoever
it went:
Noël, Noël, Noël, Noël,
Born is the King of Israel.

This star drew nigh to the north-
west;
O'er Bethlehem it took its rest;
And there it did both stop and stay
Right over the place where Jesus
lay:
Noël, Noël, Noël, Noël,
Born is the King of Israel.

Then entered in those Wise Men three,
Full reverently upon their knee,
And offered there in his presence,
Their gold and myrrh and frankincense:
Noël, Noël, Noël, Noël,
Born is the King of Israel.

Then let us all with one accord
Sing praises to our heavenly Lord
That hath made heaven and
earth of nought,
And with his blood mankind hath bought:
Noël, Noël, Noël, Noël,
Born is the King of Israel.

Which scene in White Christmas wasn't originally slated to
be in the film?
Bing Crosby and Danny Kaye singing, "Sisters"

DECEMBER 21

Today's Activities:

Things To Remember:

Christmas Song of the Day!
"Twelve Days of Christmas" Frederic Austin

On the first day of Christmas my true love sent to me
A partridge in a pear tree.

On the second day of Christmas my true love sent to me
Two turtle doves,
And a partridge in a pear tree.

On the third day of Christmas my true love sent to me
Three French hens,
Two turtle doves,
And a partridge in a pear tree.

four calling birds
five gold rings
six geese a-laying
seven swans a-swimming
eight maids a-milking
nine ladies dancing
ten lords a-leaping
eleven pipers piping
twelve drummers drumming

How many gifts in total were given in "The Twelve Days of Christmas" song?
364

DECEMBER 22

Today's Activities:

- ☐ ______________________
- ☐ ______________________
- ☐ ______________________
- ☐ ______________________
- ☐ ______________________

- ☐ ______________________
- ☐ ______________________
- ☐ ______________________
- ☐ ______________________
- ☐ ______________________

Things To Remember:

- ☐ ______________________
- ☐ ______________________
- ☐ ______________________
- ☐ ______________________
- ☐ ______________________
- ☐ ______________________

- ☐ ______________________
- ☐ ______________________
- ☐ ______________________
- ☐ ______________________
- ☐ ______________________
- ☐ ______________________

Christmas Song of the Day!
"We Three Kings" John Henry Hopkins Jr.

We Three Kings of Orient are,
Bearing gifts we traverse afar,
Field and fountain,
Moor and mountain,
Following yonder Star.

CHORUS.
O Star of Wonder, Star of Night,
Star with Royal Beauty bright,
Westward leading,
Still proceeding,
Guide us to Thy perfect Light.

Gaspard.
Born a King on Bethlehem plain,
Gold I bring to crown Him again,
King forever,
Ceasing never
Over us all to reign.
CHORUS

Melchior.
Frankincense to offer have I,
Incense owns a Deity nigh:
Prayer and praising
All men raising,
Worship Him God on High.
CHORUS

Balthazar
Myrrh is mine; its bitter perfume
Breathes a life of gathering gloom;—
Sorrowing, sighing,
Bleeding, dying,
Sealed in the stone-cold tomb.
CHORUS

Glorious now behold Him arise,
King, and God, and Sacrifice;
Heav'n sings Hallelujah:
Hallelujah the earth replies.
CHORUS

Who played George Bailey in the Christmas classic It's a Wonderful Life? Jimmy Stewart

DECEMBER 23

Today's Activities:

- [ ] ______________________
- [ ] ______________________
- [ ] ______________________
- [ ] ______________________
- [ ] ______________________

- [ ] ______________________
- [ ] ______________________
- [ ] ______________________
- [ ] ______________________
- [ ] ______________________

Things To Remember:

- [ ] ______________________
- [ ] ______________________
- [ ] ______________________
- [ ] ______________________
- [ ] ______________________
- [ ] ______________________

- [ ] ______________________
- [ ] ______________________
- [ ] ______________________
- [ ] ______________________
- [ ] ______________________
- [ ] ______________________

Christmas Song of the Day!

"Silent Night" Joseph Mohr

Silent night! Holy night!
All is calm, all is bright
Round yon virgin mother and child!
Holy infant, so tender and mild,
Sleep in heavenly peace!
Sleep in heavenly peace!

Silent night! Holy night!
Shepherds quake at the sight!
Glories stream from heaven afar,
Heavenly hosts sing Alleluia!
Christ the Saviour is born!
Christ the Saviour is born!

Silent night! Holy night!
Son of God, love's pure light
Radiant beams from thy holy face
With the dawn of redeeming grace,
Jesus, Lord, at thy birth!
Jesus, Lord, at thy birth!

Who invented electric Christmas lights?
Thomas Edison in 1880

DECEMBER 24

Today's Activities:

- [ ] ________________________
- [ ] ________________________
- [ ] ________________________
- [ ] ________________________
- [ ] ________________________

- [ ] ________________________
- [ ] ________________________
- [ ] ________________________
- [ ] ________________________
- [ ] ________________________

Things To Remember:

- [ ] ________________________
- [ ] ________________________
- [ ] ________________________
- [ ] ________________________
- [ ] ________________________

- [ ] ________________________
- [ ] ________________________
- [ ] ________________________
- [ ] ________________________
- [ ] ________________________

Christmas Song of the Day!

"O Holy Night" Placide Cappeau (English Version: John Sullivan Dwight)

O holy night!
The stars are brightly shining
It is the night of the dear Savior's birth!
Long lay the world in sin and error pining
Till he appeared and the soul felt its worth.
A thrill of hope the weary world rejoices
For yonder breaks a new and glorious morn!

Led by the light of Faith serenely beaming
With glowing hearts by His cradle we stand
So led by light of a star sweetly gleaming
Here come the wise men from Orient land
The King of kings lay thus in lowly manger
In all our trials born to be our friend.

Truly He taught us to love one another
His law is love and His gospel is peace
Chains shall He break for the slave is our brother
And in His name all oppression shall cease
Sweet hymns of joy in grateful chorus raise we,
Let all within us praise His holy name.

Fall on your knees
O hear the angel voices
O night divine
O night when Christ was born
O night divine
O night, O night divine

Fall on your knees
O hear the angel voices
O night divine
O night when Christ was born
O night divine
O night, O night divine

Fall on your knees
O hear the angel voices
O night divine
O night when Christ was born
O night divine
O night, O night divine

What is the most recorded Christmas song of all time?
"Silent Night"

DECEMBER 25

Today's Activities:

Things To Remember:

Christmas Song of the Day!
"What Child Is This?" William Chatterton Dix

What Child is this who, laid to rest
On Mary's lap is sleeping?
Whom Angels greet with anthems sweet,
While shepherds watch are keeping?

This, this is Christ the King,
Whom shepherds guard and Angels sing;
Haste, haste, to bring Him laud,
The Babe, the Son of Mary.

Why lies He in such mean estate,
Where ox and ass are feeding?
Good Christians, fear, for sinners here
The silent Word is pleading.

Nails, spear shall pierce Him through,
The cross be borne for me, for you.
Hail, hail the Word made flesh,
The Babe, the Son of Mary.

So bring Him incense, gold and myrrh,
Come peasant, king to own Him;
The King of kings salvation brings,
Let loving hearts enthrone Him.

Raise, raise a song on high,
The Virgin sings her lullaby.
Joy, joy for Christ is born,
The Babe, the Son of Mary.

What was the original title for The Little Drummer Boy?
Carol of the Drum

DECEMBER 26

Today's Activities:

- ☐ ___________________________
- ☐ ___________________________
- ☐ ___________________________
- ☐ ___________________________
- ☐ ___________________________

- ☐ ___________________________
- ☐ ___________________________
- ☐ ___________________________
- ☐ ___________________________
- ☐ ___________________________

Things To Remember:

- ☐ ___________________________
- ☐ ___________________________
- ☐ ___________________________
- ☐ ___________________________
- ☐ ___________________________
- ☐ ___________________________

- ☐ ___________________________
- ☐ ___________________________
- ☐ ___________________________
- ☐ ___________________________
- ☐ ___________________________
- ☐ ___________________________

Christmas Song of the Day!
"Deck The Halls" Thomas Oliphant (translation)

Deck the hall with boughs of holly,
Fa, la, la, la, la, la, la, la, la!
'Tis the season to be jolly,
Fa, la, la, la, la, la, la, la, la!
Don we now our gay apparel,
Fa, la, la, la, la, la, la, la!
Troul the ancient Christmas carol,
Fa, la, la, la, la, la, la, la!

See the blazing yule before us,
Fa, la, la, la, la, la, la, la, la!
Strike the harp and join the chorus.
Fa, la, la, la, la, la, la, la, la!
Follow me in merry measure,
Fa, la, la, la, la, la, la, la!
While I tell of Christmas treasure,
Fa, la, la, la, la, la, la, la, la!

Fast away the old year passes,
Fa, la, la, la, la, la, la, la, la!
Hail the new, ye lads and lasses!
Fa, la, la, la, la, la, la, la, la!
Sing we joyousall together,
Fa, la, la, la, la, la, la, la!
Heedless of the wind and weather,
Fa, la, la, la, la, la, la, la, la!

What would you be drinking if you had 'Glühwein?'
Mulled wine

DECEMBER 27

Today's Activities:

Things To Remember:

Christmas Song of the Day!
"Jesu, Joy of Man's Desiring" arr. By Robert Bridges

Jesu, joy of man's desiring,
Holy wisdom, love most bright;
Drawn by Thee, our souls aspiring
Soar to uncreated light.

Word of God, our flesh that fashioned,
With the fire of life impassioned,
Striving still to truth unknown,
Soaring, dying round Thy throne.

Through the way where hope is guiding,
Hark, what peaceful music rings;
Where the flock, in Thee confiding,
Drink of joy from deathless springs.

Theirs is beauty's fairest pleasure;
Theirs is wisdom's holiest treasure.
Thou dost ever lead Thine own
In the love of joys unknown.

In which direction should you stir mincemeat for good luck?
Clockwise

DECEMBER 28

Today's Activities:

Things To Remember:

Christmas Song of the Day!
"Toyland" Mel Leven and Glen MacDonough

Toyland, Toyland,
Dear little girl and boy land
While you dwell within it
You are ever happy there

Toyland, Toyland,
We're on our way to Toyland
Don't know when we'll get there
But we know there's fun in store

Childhood's toyland
Wonderful world of joyland
Wouldn't it be fine if
We could stay there forevermore

Toyland, Toyland,
Wonderful girl and boy land
Once you leave its borders
You can never return again

What well-known Christmas carol became the first song ever
broadcast from space in 1965?
Jingle Bells

DECEMBER 29

Today's Activities:

☐ _______________________   ☐ _______________________
☐ _______________________   ☐ _______________________
☐ _______________________   ☐ _______________________
☐ _______________________   ☐ _______________________
☐ _______________________   ☐ _______________________

Things To Remember:

☐ _______________________   ☐ _______________________
☐ _______________________   ☐ _______________________
☐ _______________________   ☐ _______________________
☐ _______________________   ☐ _______________________
☐ _______________________   ☐ _______________________
☐ _______________________   ☐ _______________________

Christmas Song of the Day!

"Wassail Song" Unknown

Here we come a-wassailing
Among the leaves so green,
Here we come a-wand'ring
So fair to be seen.
Love and joy come to you,
And to you your wassail, too,
And God bless you, and send you
A Happy New Year,
And God send you a Happy New Year.

We are not daily beggers
That beg from door to door,
But we are neighbors' children
Whom you have seen before
Love and joy come to you,
And to you your wassail, too,
And God bless you, and send you
A Happy New Year,
And God send you a Happy New Year.

Good master and good mistress,
As you sit beside the fire,
Pray think of us poor children
Who wander in the mire.
Love and joy come to you,
And to you your wassail, too,
And God bless you, and send you
A Happy New Year,
And God send you a Happy New Year

We have a little purse
Made of ratching leather skin;
We want some of your small change
To line it well within.
Love and joy come to you,
And to you your wassail, too,
And God bless you, and send you
A Happy New Year,
And God send you a Happy New Year.

Bring us out a table
And spread it with a cloth;
Bring us out a cheese,
And of your Christmas loaf.
Love and joy come to you,
And to you your wassail, too,
And God bless you, and send you
A Happy New Year,
And God send you a Happy New Year.

God bless the master of this house,
Likewise the mistress too;
And all the little children
That round the table go.
Love and joy come to you,
And to you your wassail, too,
And God bless you, and send you
A Happy New Year,
And God send you a Happy New Year.

Bob Fosse, a famous choreographer, was uncredited on "White Christmas"

DECEMBER 30

Today's Activities:

☐ __________________________ ☐ __________________________
☐ __________________________ ☐ __________________________
☐ __________________________ ☐ __________________________
☐ __________________________ ☐ __________________________
☐ __________________________ ☐ __________________________

Things To Remember:

☐ __________________________ ☐ __________________________
☐ __________________________ ☐ __________________________
☐ __________________________ ☐ __________________________
☐ __________________________ ☐ __________________________
☐ __________________________ ☐ __________________________

Christmas Song of the Day!

"(O Tannenbaum) O Christmas Tree" Ernst Anschütz

O Christmas tree, o Christmas tree
Thy leaves are so unchanging
O Christmas tree, o Christmas tree
Thy leaves are so unchanging
Not only green when summer's here
But also when it's cold and drear
O Christmas tree, o Christmas tree
Thy leaves are so unchanging

O Christmas tree, o Christmas tree
Such pleasure do you bring me
O Christmas tree, o Christmas tree
Such pleasure do you bring me

For every year this Christmas tree
Brings to us such joy and glee
O Christmas tree, o Christmas tree
Such pleasure do you bring me

O Christmas tree, o Christmas tree
You'll ever be unchanging
A symbol of goodwill and love
You'll ever be unchanging

Each shining light, each silver bell
No one alive spreads cheer so well
O Christmas tree, o Christmas tree
You'll ever be unchanging

What Christmas-themed ballet premiered in Saint Petersburg, Russia in 1892?

The Nutcracker

DECEMBER 31

Today's Activities:

- ☐ ___________________
- ☐ ___________________
- ☐ ___________________
- ☐ ___________________
- ☐ ___________________

- ☐ ___________________
- ☐ ___________________
- ☐ ___________________
- ☐ ___________________
- ☐ ___________________

Things To Remember:

- ☐ ___________________
- ☐ ___________________
- ☐ ___________________
- ☐ ___________________
- ☐ ___________________
- ☐ ___________________

- ☐ ___________________
- ☐ ___________________
- ☐ ___________________
- ☐ ___________________
- ☐ ___________________
- ☐ ___________________

Christmas Song of the Day!
"Auld Lang Syne" Robert Burns

Should old acquaintance be
forgot,
and never brought to mind?
Should old acquaintance be
forgot,
and auld lang syne?

Chorus:

For auld lang syne, my dear,
for auld lang syne,
we'll take a cup of kindness
yet,
for auld lang syne.

And surely you'll buy
your pint cup!
and surely I'll buy mine!
And we'll take a cup o'
kindness yet,
for auld lang syne.
Chorus

We two have run about
the hills,
and picked the daisies
fine;
But we've wandered
many a weary foot,
since auld lang syne.

Chorus

We two have paddled in the
stream,
from morning sun till dine;
But seas between us broad
have roared
since auld lang syne.

Chrous

And there's a hand my trusty
friend!
And give me a hand o' thine!
And we'll take a right good-
will draught,
for auld lang syne.

Chorus

The Netherlands has the tradition of filling children's clogs
with candy and treats on December 5!

A Year of Firsts
Part One
By Rebecca M. Norris

"**No**, sweetheart," he said, despondently. "I just can't. Not this year. Maybe next year. I'll talk to you later."

He hung up the phone. This had been an incredibly difficult year. His Year of Firsts, as his pastor called it. The very first year after a loved one dies. The first New Year's without them. The first Valentine's Day. The first birthday. The first anniversary… The first time every event comes around and one has to celebrate alone. He hated the Year of Firsts, but it was almost over. This was the first Christmas without his beloved. If he could make it through this season, his Year of Firsts will be over. Finally over. Maybe then, he could heal.

She meant everything to him. His beloved. They had known each other since they were two years old, and played together in the church nursery. They went to the same preschool, elementary school, junior high, but not high school. Her family had moved away at the beginning of high school, but they kept in touch. They were the very best of friends their entire lives. When college graduation came, he was right there cheering her on. It was only natural that he propose to her soon after. He loved her so.

"Thirty-five years married to the most incredible woman I have ever known," he sighed. "Not nearly long enough." He rose from his chair and looked at the calendar. Christmas was only two days away. He just had to make it through Christmas Day and it would be over.

She died on Christmas Day. He didn't want to face it. *Can't I just sleep through that day, Lord*, he prayed. As usual these days, he couldn't hear God's reply.

He climbed the stairs and entered the bedroom he and his beloved had shared. He hadn't slept in it since the day she left without him. He couldn't. The room carried her presence, just like the entire house did. Everywhere he looked, there was his beloved. But he couldn't bear the thought of someone else living in her house. He would stay here until it was his time to join her, and pass the house on to one of the kids.

To Be Continued

For Gifts Given

In Your Heart
By Scott Norris

To the one with borrowed gifts
May your joy not end or start
As you begin to know that
Christmas is in each one's heart

To the one who can share goods
May your charity refresh
As Christmas exists within
Each one with a heart and flesh

To the one who is far off
May you know much hope and love
As Christmas serves to tell us
Of He who came from above

To the one who will read this
May your outlook not depart
From things unforgettable
As Christmas is in your heart

Christmas Gift Tracker

Name: _________________________________

Address: _______________________________

____

City, State, ZIP: _________________________

(Tape Receipt Here)

Gift Given & Amount: _____________________

Mailed Via: _____________________________

Date Mailed: ____________________________

Tracking Number: ________________________

Date Received: ___________________________

Name: _________________________________

Address: _______________________________

____

City, State, ZIP: _________________________

(Tape Receipt Here)

Gift Given & Amount: _____________________

Mailed Via: _____________________________

Date Mailed: ____________________________

Tracking Number: ________________________

Date Received: ___________________________

Name: _________________________________

Address: _______________________________

____

City, State, ZIP: _________________________

(Tape Receipt Here)

Gift Given & Amount: _____________________

Mailed Via: _____________________________

Date Mailed: ____________________________

Tracking Number: ________________________

Date Received: ___________________________

Christmas Gift Tracker

Name: _________________________________
Address: _______________________________
____
City, State, ZIP: ________________________

(Tape Receipt
Here)

Gift Given & Amount: ____________________
Mailed Via: _____________________________
Date Mailed: ____________________________
Tracking Number: ________________________
Date Received: __________________________

Name: _________________________________
Address: _______________________________
____
City, State, ZIP: ________________________

(Tape Receipt
Here)

Gift Given & Amount: ____________________
Mailed Via: _____________________________
Date Mailed: ____________________________
Tracking Number: ________________________
Date Received: __________________________

Name: _________________________________
Address: _______________________________
____
City, State, ZIP: ________________________

(Tape Receipt
Here)

Gift Given & Amount: ____________________
Mailed Via: _____________________________
Date Mailed: ____________________________
Tracking Number: ________________________
Date Received: __________________________

Christmas Gift Tracker

Name: ______________________________
Address: ____________________________
____
City, State, ZIP: ____________________

Gift Given & Amount: ________________
Mailed Via: _________________________
Date Mailed: ________________________
Tracking Number: ____________________
Date Received: ______________________

(Tape Receipt Here)

Name: ______________________________
Address: ____________________________
____
City, State, ZIP: ____________________

Gift Given & Amount: ________________
Mailed Via: _________________________
Date Mailed: ________________________
Tracking Number: ____________________
Date Received: ______________________

(Tape Receipt Here)

Name: ______________________________
Address: ____________________________
____
City, State, ZIP: ____________________

Gift Given & Amount: ________________
Mailed Via: _________________________
Date Mailed: ________________________
Tracking Number: ____________________
Date Received: ______________________

(Tape Receipt Here)

Christmas Gift Tracker

Name: _______________________________
Address: _____________________________
____
City, State, ZIP: _____________________

(Tape Receipt Here)

Gift Given & Amount: _________________
Mailed Via: __________________________
Date Mailed: _________________________
Tracking Number: _____________________
Date Received: _______________________

Name: _______________________________
Address: _____________________________
____
City, State, ZIP: _____________________

(Tape Receipt Here)

Gift Given & Amount: _________________
Mailed Via: __________________________
Date Mailed: _________________________
Tracking Number: _____________________
Date Received: _______________________

Name: _______________________________
Address: _____________________________
____
City, State, ZIP: _____________________

(Tape Receipt Here)

Gift Given & Amount: _________________
Mailed Via: __________________________
Date Mailed: _________________________
Tracking Number: _____________________
Date Received: _______________________

Christmas Gift Tracker

Name: _______________________________

Address: _______________________________

____

City, State, ZIP: _______________________________

(Tape Receipt Here)

Gift Given & Amount: _______________________________

Mailed Via: _______________________________

Date Mailed: _______________________________

Tracking Number: _______________________________

Date Received: _______________________________

Name: _______________________________

Address: _______________________________

____

City, State, ZIP: _______________________________

(Tape Receipt Here)

Gift Given & Amount: _______________________________

Mailed Via: _______________________________

Date Mailed: _______________________________

Tracking Number: _______________________________

Date Received: _______________________________

Name: _______________________________

Address: _______________________________

____

City, State, ZIP: _______________________________

(Tape Receipt Here)

Gift Given & Amount: _______________________________

Mailed Via: _______________________________

Date Mailed: _______________________________

Tracking Number: _______________________________

Date Received: _______________________________

Christmas Gift Tracker

Name: _______________________________
Address: _______________________________
____
City, State, ZIP: _______________________________

(Tape Receipt Here)

Gift Given & Amount: _______________________
Mailed Via: _______________________________
Date Mailed: _______________________________
Tracking Number: _______________________________
Date Received: _______________________________

Name: _______________________________
Address: _______________________________
____
City, State, ZIP: _______________________________

(Tape Receipt Here)

Gift Given & Amount: _______________________
Mailed Via: _______________________________
Date Mailed: _______________________________
Tracking Number: _______________________________
Date Received: _______________________________

Name: _______________________________
Address: _______________________________
____
City, State, ZIP: _______________________________

(Tape Receipt Here)

Gift Given & Amount: _______________________
Mailed Via: _______________________________
Date Mailed: _______________________________
Tracking Number: _______________________________
Date Received: _______________________________

Christmas Gift Tracker

Name: _________________________________
Address: _______________________________
____
City, State, ZIP: _________________________

(Tape Receipt Here)

Gift Given & Amount: ____________________
Mailed Via: _____________________________
Date Mailed: ____________________________
Tracking Number: _______________________
Date Received: __________________________

Name: _________________________________
Address: _______________________________
____
City, State, ZIP: _________________________

(Tape Receipt Here)

Gift Given & Amount: ____________________
Mailed Via: _____________________________
Date Mailed: ____________________________
Tracking Number: _______________________
Date Received: __________________________

Name: _________________________________
Address: _______________________________
____
City, State, ZIP: _________________________

(Tape Receipt Here)

Gift Given & Amount: ____________________
Mailed Via: _____________________________
Date Mailed: ____________________________
Tracking Number: _______________________
Date Received: __________________________

Christmas Gift Tracker

Name: _______________________________
Address: _______________________________
____
City, State, ZIP: _______________________________

(Tape Receipt Here)

Gift Given & Amount: _______________________________
Mailed Via: _______________________________
Date Mailed: _______________________________
Tracking Number: _______________________________
Date Received: _______________________________

Name: _______________________________
Address: _______________________________
____
City, State, ZIP: _______________________________

(Tape Receipt Here)

Gift Given & Amount: _______________________________
Mailed Via: _______________________________
Date Mailed: _______________________________
Tracking Number: _______________________________
Date Received: _______________________________

Name: _______________________________
Address: _______________________________
____
City, State, ZIP: _______________________________

(Tape Receipt Here)

Gift Given & Amount: _______________________________
Mailed Via: _______________________________
Date Mailed: _______________________________
Tracking Number: _______________________________
Date Received: _______________________________

Christmas Gift Tracker

Name: _______________________________
Address: _____________________________
____
City, State, ZIP: _____________________

(Tape Receipt Here)

Gift Given & Amount: __________________
Mailed Via: __________________________
Date Mailed: _________________________
Tracking Number: _____________________
Date Received: _______________________

Name: _______________________________
Address: _____________________________
____
City, State, ZIP: _____________________

(Tape Receipt Here)

Gift Given & Amount: __________________
Mailed Via: __________________________
Date Mailed: _________________________
Tracking Number: _____________________
Date Received: _______________________

Name: _______________________________
Address: _____________________________
____
City, State, ZIP: _____________________

(Tape Receipt Here)

Gift Given & Amount: __________________
Mailed Via: __________________________
Date Mailed: _________________________
Tracking Number: _____________________
Date Received: _______________________

Christmas Gift Tracker

Name: _______________________________
Address: _____________________________
____
City, State, ZIP: _____________________

(Tape Receipt Here)

Gift Given & Amount: _________________
Mailed Via: __________________________
Date Mailed: _________________________
Tracking Number: _____________________
Date Received: _______________________

Name: _______________________________
Address: _____________________________
____
City, State, ZIP: _____________________

(Tape Receipt Here)

Gift Given & Amount: _________________
Mailed Via: __________________________
Date Mailed: _________________________
Tracking Number: _____________________
Date Received: _______________________

Name: _______________________________
Address: _____________________________
____
City, State, ZIP: _____________________

(Tape Receipt Here)

Gift Given & Amount: _________________
Mailed Via: __________________________
Date Mailed: _________________________
Tracking Number: _____________________
Date Received: _______________________

Christmas Gift Tracker

Name: _______________________________
Address: _____________________________
____
City, State, ZIP: _____________________

(Tape Receipt Here)

Gift Given & Amount: _________________
Mailed Via: __________________________
Date Mailed: _________________________
Tracking Number: _____________________
Date Received: _______________________

Name: _______________________________
Address: _____________________________
____
City, State, ZIP: _____________________

(Tape Receipt Here)

Gift Given & Amount: _________________
Mailed Via: __________________________
Date Mailed: _________________________
Tracking Number: _____________________
Date Received: _______________________

Name: _______________________________
Address: _____________________________
____
City, State, ZIP: _____________________

(Tape Receipt Here)

Gift Given & Amount: _________________
Mailed Via: __________________________
Date Mailed: _________________________
Tracking Number: _____________________
Date Received: _______________________

Christmas Gift Tracker

Name: ______________________________
Address: ____________________________
____
City, State, ZIP: ____________________

(Tape Receipt Here)

Gift Given & Amount: _________________
Mailed Via: __________________________
Date Mailed: _________________________
Tracking Number: _____________________
Date Received: _______________________

Name: ______________________________
Address: ____________________________
____
City, State, ZIP: ____________________

(Tape Receipt Here)

Gift Given & Amount: _________________
Mailed Via: __________________________
Date Mailed: _________________________
Tracking Number: _____________________
Date Received: _______________________

Name: ______________________________
Address: ____________________________
____
City, State, ZIP: ____________________

(Tape Receipt Here)

Gift Given & Amount: _________________
Mailed Via: __________________________
Date Mailed: _________________________
Tracking Number: _____________________
Date Received: _______________________

Christmas Gift Tracker

Name: _______________________________
Address: _______________________________
____
City, State, ZIP: _______________________________

(Tape Receipt Here)

Gift Given & Amount: _______________________
Mailed Via: _______________________________
Date Mailed: _______________________________
Tracking Number: _______________________
Date Received: _______________________________

Name: _______________________________
Address: _______________________________
____
City, State, ZIP: _______________________________

(Tape Receipt Here)

Gift Given & Amount: _______________________
Mailed Via: _______________________________
Date Mailed: _______________________________
Tracking Number: _______________________
Date Received: _______________________________

Name: _______________________________
Address: _______________________________
____
City, State, ZIP: _______________________________

(Tape Receipt Here)

Gift Given & Amount: _______________________
Mailed Via: _______________________________
Date Mailed: _______________________________
Tracking Number: _______________________
Date Received: _______________________________

Christmas Gift Tracker

Name: _______________________________
Address: _______________________________
____
City, State, ZIP: _______________________________

(Tape Receipt Here)

Gift Given & Amount: _______________________
Mailed Via: _______________________________
Date Mailed: _______________________________
Tracking Number: _______________________
Date Received: _______________________________

Name: _______________________________
Address: _______________________________
____
City, State, ZIP: _______________________________

(Tape Receipt Here)

Gift Given & Amount: _______________________
Mailed Via: _______________________________
Date Mailed: _______________________________
Tracking Number: _______________________
Date Received: _______________________________

Name: _______________________________
Address: _______________________________
____
City, State, ZIP: _______________________________

(Tape Receipt Here)

Gift Given & Amount: _______________________
Mailed Via: _______________________________
Date Mailed: _______________________________
Tracking Number: _______________________
Date Received: _______________________________

Christmas Gift Tracker

Name: _______________________________
Address: _____________________________
____
City, State, ZIP: _______________________

(Tape Receipt Here)

Gift Given & Amount: ___________________
Mailed Via: ___________________________
Date Mailed: __________________________
Tracking Number: ______________________
Date Received: ________________________

Name: _______________________________
Address: _____________________________
____
City, State, ZIP: _______________________

(Tape Receipt Here)

Gift Given & Amount: ___________________
Mailed Via: ___________________________
Date Mailed: __________________________
Tracking Number: ______________________
Date Received: ________________________

Name: _______________________________
Address: _____________________________
____
City, State, ZIP: _______________________

(Tape Receipt Here)

Gift Given & Amount: ___________________
Mailed Via: ___________________________
Date Mailed: __________________________
Tracking Number: ______________________
Date Received: ________________________

Christmas Gift Tracker

Name: _______________________________
Address: _____________________________
____
City, State, ZIP: ______________________

(Tape Receipt Here)

Gift Given & Amount: __________________
Mailed Via: ___________________________
Date Mailed: _________________________
Tracking Number: _____________________
Date Received: _______________________

Name: _______________________________
Address: _____________________________
____
City, State, ZIP: ______________________

(Tape Receipt Here)

Gift Given & Amount: __________________
Mailed Via: ___________________________
Date Mailed: _________________________
Tracking Number: _____________________
Date Received: _______________________

Name: _______________________________
Address: _____________________________
____
City, State, ZIP: ______________________

(Tape Receipt Here)

Gift Given & Amount: __________________
Mailed Via: ___________________________
Date Mailed: _________________________
Tracking Number: _____________________
Date Received: _______________________

Christmas Gift Tracker

Name: _______________________________
Address: _____________________________
____
City, State, ZIP: _______________________

(Tape Receipt Here)

Gift Given & Amount: __________________
Mailed Via: _________________________
Date Mailed: ________________________
Tracking Number: ____________________
Date Received: ______________________

Name: _______________________________
Address: _____________________________
____
City, State, ZIP: _______________________

(Tape Receipt Here)

Gift Given & Amount: __________________
Mailed Via: _________________________
Date Mailed: ________________________
Tracking Number: ____________________
Date Received: ______________________

Name: _______________________________
Address: _____________________________
____
City, State, ZIP: _______________________

(Tape Receipt Here)

Gift Given & Amount: __________________
Mailed Via: _________________________
Date Mailed: ________________________
Tracking Number: ____________________
Date Received: ______________________

Christmas Gift Tracker

Name: _______________________________
Address: _______________________________
____
City, State, ZIP: _______________________________

(Tape Receipt Here)

Gift Given & Amount: _______________________
Mailed Via: _______________________________
Date Mailed: _______________________________
Tracking Number: _______________________
Date Received: _______________________________

Name: _______________________________
Address: _______________________________
____
City, State, ZIP: _______________________________

(Tape Receipt Here)

Gift Given & Amount: _______________________
Mailed Via: _______________________________
Date Mailed: _______________________________
Tracking Number: _______________________
Date Received: _______________________________

Name: _______________________________
Address: _______________________________
____
City, State, ZIP: _______________________________

(Tape Receipt Here)

Gift Given & Amount: _______________________
Mailed Via: _______________________________
Date Mailed: _______________________________
Tracking Number: _______________________
Date Received: _______________________________

Christmas Gift Tracker

Name: _______________________________
Address: _____________________________
____
City, State, ZIP: _____________________

(Tape Receipt Here)

Gift Given & Amount: _________________
Mailed Via: __________________________
Date Mailed: _________________________
Tracking Number: _____________________
Date Received: _______________________

Name: _______________________________
Address: _____________________________
____
City, State, ZIP: _____________________

(Tape Receipt Here)

Gift Given & Amount: _________________
Mailed Via: __________________________
Date Mailed: _________________________
Tracking Number: _____________________
Date Received: _______________________

Name: _______________________________
Address: _____________________________
____
City, State, ZIP: _____________________

(Tape Receipt Here)

Gift Given & Amount: _________________
Mailed Via: __________________________
Date Mailed: _________________________
Tracking Number: _____________________
Date Received: _______________________

Christmas Gift Tracker

Name: _______________________________

Address: _______________________________

____

City, State, ZIP: _______________________________

(Tape Receipt Here)

Gift Given & Amount: _______________________

Mailed Via: _______________________________

Date Mailed: _______________________________

Tracking Number: _______________________________

Date Received: _______________________________

Name: _______________________________

Address: _______________________________

____

City, State, ZIP: _______________________________

(Tape Receipt Here)

Gift Given & Amount: _______________________

Mailed Via: _______________________________

Date Mailed: _______________________________

Tracking Number: _______________________________

Date Received: _______________________________

Name: _______________________________

Address: _______________________________

____

City, State, ZIP: _______________________________

(Tape Receipt Here)

Gift Given & Amount: _______________________

Mailed Via: _______________________________

Date Mailed: _______________________________

Tracking Number: _______________________________

Date Received: _______________________________

Christmas Gift Tracker

Name: _________________________________
Address: _______________________________
____
City, State, ZIP: _________________________

(Tape Receipt Here)

Gift Given & Amount: ____________________
Mailed Via: _____________________________
Date Mailed: ____________________________
Tracking Number: ________________________
Date Received: __________________________

Name: _________________________________
Address: _______________________________
____
City, State, ZIP: _________________________

(Tape Receipt Here)

Gift Given & Amount: ____________________
Mailed Via: _____________________________
Date Mailed: ____________________________
Tracking Number: ________________________
Date Received: __________________________

Name: _________________________________
Address: _______________________________
____
City, State, ZIP: _________________________

(Tape Receipt Here)

Gift Given & Amount: ____________________
Mailed Via: _____________________________
Date Mailed: ____________________________
Tracking Number: ________________________
Date Received: __________________________

Christmas Gift Tracker

Name: ___________________________________
Address: ________________________________
____
City, State, ZIP: ________________________

Gift Given & Amount: ___________________
Mailed Via: _____________________________
Date Mailed: ____________________________
Tracking Number: _______________________
Date Received: __________________________

(Tape Receipt Here)

Name: ___________________________________
Address: ________________________________
____
City, State, ZIP: ________________________

Gift Given & Amount: ___________________
Mailed Via: _____________________________
Date Mailed: ____________________________
Tracking Number: _______________________
Date Received: __________________________

(Tape Receipt Here)

Name: ___________________________________
Address: ________________________________
____
City, State, ZIP: ________________________

Gift Given & Amount: ___________________
Mailed Via: _____________________________
Date Mailed: ____________________________
Tracking Number: _______________________
Date Received: __________________________

(Tape Receipt Here)

Christmas Gift Tracker

Name: _______________________________

Address: _____________________________

____

City, State, ZIP: _______________________

Gift Given & Amount: ___________________

Mailed Via: ___________________________

Date Mailed: _________________________

Tracking Number: ______________________

Date Received: _______________________

(Tape Receipt Here)

Name: _______________________________

Address: _____________________________

____

City, State, ZIP: _______________________

Gift Given & Amount: ___________________

Mailed Via: ___________________________

Date Mailed: _________________________

Tracking Number: ______________________

Date Received: _______________________

(Tape Receipt Here)

Name: _______________________________

Address: _____________________________

____

City, State, ZIP: _______________________

Gift Given & Amount: ___________________

Mailed Via: ___________________________

Date Mailed: _________________________

Tracking Number: ______________________

Date Received: _______________________

(Tape Receipt Here)

Christmas Gift Tracker

Name: _______________________________
Address: _____________________________
____
City, State, ZIP: ______________________

(Tape Receipt Here)

Gift Given & Amount: _________________
Mailed Via: __________________________
Date Mailed: _________________________
Tracking Number: _____________________
Date Received: _______________________

Name: _______________________________
Address: _____________________________
____
City, State, ZIP: ______________________

(Tape Receipt Here)

Gift Given & Amount: _________________
Mailed Via: __________________________
Date Mailed: _________________________
Tracking Number: _____________________
Date Received: _______________________

Name: _______________________________
Address: _____________________________
____
City, State, ZIP: ______________________

(Tape Receipt Here)

Gift Given & Amount: _________________
Mailed Via: __________________________
Date Mailed: _________________________
Tracking Number: _____________________
Date Received: _______________________

Christmas Gift Tracker

Name: _______________________________
Address: _____________________________
____
City, State, ZIP: _______________________

(Tape Receipt Here)

Gift Given & Amount: _________________
Mailed Via: __________________________
Date Mailed: _________________________
Tracking Number: _____________________
Date Received: _______________________

Name: _______________________________
Address: _____________________________
____
City, State, ZIP: _______________________

(Tape Receipt Here)

Gift Given & Amount: _________________
Mailed Via: __________________________
Date Mailed: _________________________
Tracking Number: _____________________
Date Received: _______________________

Name: _______________________________
Address: _____________________________
____
City, State, ZIP: _______________________

(Tape Receipt Here)

Gift Given & Amount: _________________
Mailed Via: __________________________
Date Mailed: _________________________
Tracking Number: _____________________
Date Received: _______________________

Christmas Gift Tracker

Name: _______________________________
Address: _______________________________
____
City, State, ZIP: _______________________________

Gift Given & Amount: _______________________
Mailed Via: _______________________________
Date Mailed: _______________________________
Tracking Number: _______________________
Date Received: _______________________________

Name: _______________________________
Address: _______________________________
____
City, State, ZIP: _______________________________

Gift Given & Amount: _______________________
Mailed Via: _______________________________
Date Mailed: _______________________________
Tracking Number: _______________________
Date Received: _______________________________

Name: _______________________________
Address: _______________________________
____
City, State, ZIP: _______________________________

Gift Given & Amount: _______________________
Mailed Via: _______________________________
Date Mailed: _______________________________
Tracking Number: _______________________
Date Received: _______________________________

Christmas Gift Tracker

Name: _______________________________
Address: _______________________________
____
City, State, ZIP: _______________________________

Gift Given & Amount: _______________________
Mailed Via: _______________________________
Date Mailed: _______________________________
Tracking Number: _______________________
Date Received: _______________________

(Tape Receipt Here)

Name: _______________________________
Address: _______________________________
____
City, State, ZIP: _______________________________

Gift Given & Amount: _______________________
Mailed Via: _______________________________
Date Mailed: _______________________________
Tracking Number: _______________________
Date Received: _______________________

(Tape Receipt Here)

Name: _______________________________
Address: _______________________________
____
City, State, ZIP: _______________________________

Gift Given & Amount: _______________________
Mailed Via: _______________________________
Date Mailed: _______________________________
Tracking Number: _______________________
Date Received: _______________________

(Tape Receipt Here)

Christmas Gift Tracker

Name: _______________________________
Address: _____________________________
____
City, State, ZIP: _____________________

(Tape Receipt Here)

Gift Given & Amount: _________________
Mailed Via: __________________________
Date Mailed: _________________________
Tracking Number: _____________________
Date Received: _______________________

Name: _______________________________
Address: _____________________________
____
City, State, ZIP: _____________________

(Tape Receipt Here)

Gift Given & Amount: _________________
Mailed Via: __________________________
Date Mailed: _________________________
Tracking Number: _____________________
Date Received: _______________________

Name: _______________________________
Address: _____________________________
____
City, State, ZIP: _____________________

(Tape Receipt Here)

Gift Given & Amount: _________________
Mailed Via: __________________________
Date Mailed: _________________________
Tracking Number: _____________________
Date Received: _______________________

Christmas Gift Tracker

Name: _______________________________

Address: _______________________________

____

City, State, ZIP: _______________________________

(Tape Receipt Here)

Gift Given & Amount: _______________________

Mailed Via: _______________________________

Date Mailed: _______________________________

Tracking Number: _______________________

Date Received: _______________________________

Name: _______________________________

Address: _______________________________

____

City, State, ZIP: _______________________________

(Tape Receipt Here)

Gift Given & Amount: _______________________

Mailed Via: _______________________________

Date Mailed: _______________________________

Tracking Number: _______________________

Date Received: _______________________________

Name: _______________________________

Address: _______________________________

____

City, State, ZIP: _______________________________

(Tape Receipt Here)

Gift Given & Amount: _______________________

Mailed Via: _______________________________

Date Mailed: _______________________________

Tracking Number: _______________________

Date Received: _______________________________

Christmas Gift Tracker

Name: _______________________________
Address: _____________________________
____
City, State, ZIP: _____________________

(Tape Receipt Here)

Gift Given & Amount: _________________
Mailed Via: __________________________
Date Mailed: _________________________
Tracking Number: _____________________
Date Received: _______________________

____

Name: _______________________________
Address: _____________________________
____
City, State, ZIP: _____________________

(Tape Receipt Here)

Gift Given & Amount: _________________
Mailed Via: __________________________
Date Mailed: _________________________
Tracking Number: _____________________
Date Received: _______________________

____

Name: _______________________________
Address: _____________________________
____
City, State, ZIP: _____________________

(Tape Receipt Here)

Gift Given & Amount: _________________
Mailed Via: __________________________
Date Mailed: _________________________
Tracking Number: _____________________
Date Received: _______________________

Christmas Gift Tracker

Name: ______________________________
Address: ____________________________
____
City, State, ZIP: ____________________

(Tape Receipt Here)

Gift Given & Amount: ________________
Mailed Via: _________________________
Date Mailed: ________________________
Tracking Number: ____________________
Date Received: ______________________

Name: ______________________________
Address: ____________________________
____
City, State, ZIP: ____________________

(Tape Receipt Here)

Gift Given & Amount: ________________
Mailed Via: _________________________
Date Mailed: ________________________
Tracking Number: ____________________
Date Received: ______________________

Name: ______________________________
Address: ____________________________
____
City, State, ZIP: ____________________

(Tape Receipt Here)

Gift Given & Amount: ________________
Mailed Via: _________________________
Date Mailed: ________________________
Tracking Number: ____________________
Date Received: ______________________

Christmas Gift Tracker

Name: _______________________________________

Address: _____________________________________

____

City, State, ZIP: _____________________________

Gift Given & Amount: _________________________

Mailed Via: __________________________________

Date Mailed: _________________________________

Tracking Number: _____________________________

Date Received: _______________________________

(Tape Receipt Here)

Name: _______________________________________

Address: _____________________________________

____

City, State, ZIP: _____________________________

Gift Given & Amount: _________________________

Mailed Via: __________________________________

Date Mailed: _________________________________

Tracking Number: _____________________________

Date Received: _______________________________

(Tape Receipt Here)

Name: _______________________________________

Address: _____________________________________

____

City, State, ZIP: _____________________________

Gift Given & Amount: _________________________

Mailed Via: __________________________________

Date Mailed: _________________________________

Tracking Number: _____________________________

Date Received: _______________________________

(Tape Receipt Here)

Christmas Gift Tracker

Name: _______________________________

Address: _______________________________

____

City, State, ZIP: _______________________________

(Tape Receipt Here)

Gift Given & Amount: _______________________________

Mailed Via: _______________________________

Date Mailed: _______________________________

Tracking Number: _______________________________

Date Received: _______________________________

Name: _______________________________

Address: _______________________________

____

City, State, ZIP: _______________________________

(Tape Receipt Here)

Gift Given & Amount: _______________________________

Mailed Via: _______________________________

Date Mailed: _______________________________

Tracking Number: _______________________________

Date Received: _______________________________

Name: _______________________________

Address: _______________________________

____

City, State, ZIP: _______________________________

(Tape Receipt Here)

Gift Given & Amount: _______________________________

Mailed Via: _______________________________

Date Mailed: _______________________________

Tracking Number: _______________________________

Date Received: _______________________________

Christmas Gift Tracker

Name: ____________________________________
Address: __________________________________
____
City, State, ZIP: ____________________________

(Tape Receipt
Here)

Gift Given & Amount: ______________________
Mailed Via: ________________________________
Date Mailed: ______________________________
Tracking Number: __________________________
Date Received: ____________________________

Name: ____________________________________
Address: __________________________________
____
City, State, ZIP: ____________________________

(Tape Receipt
Here)

Gift Given & Amount: ______________________
Mailed Via: ________________________________
Date Mailed: ______________________________
Tracking Number: __________________________
Date Received: ____________________________

Name: ____________________________________
Address: __________________________________
____
City, State, ZIP: ____________________________

(Tape Receipt
Here)

Gift Given & Amount: ______________________
Mailed Via: ________________________________
Date Mailed: ______________________________
Tracking Number: __________________________
Date Received: ____________________________

Christmas Gift Tracker

Name: _______________________________
Address: _______________________________
____
City, State, ZIP: _______________________________

(Tape Receipt Here)

Gift Given & Amount: _______________________
Mailed Via: _______________________________
Date Mailed: _______________________________
Tracking Number: _______________________________
Date Received: _______________________________

Name: _______________________________
Address: _______________________________
____
City, State, ZIP: _______________________________

(Tape Receipt Here)

Gift Given & Amount: _______________________
Mailed Via: _______________________________
Date Mailed: _______________________________
Tracking Number: _______________________________
Date Received: _______________________________

Name: _______________________________
Address: _______________________________
____
City, State, ZIP: _______________________________

(Tape Receipt Here)

Gift Given & Amount: _______________________
Mailed Via: _______________________________
Date Mailed: _______________________________
Tracking Number: _______________________________
Date Received: _______________________________

Christmas Gift Tracker

Name: ___________________________________

Address: _________________________________

____

City, State, ZIP: __________________________

(Tape Receipt Here)

Gift Given & Amount: ______________________

Mailed Via: ______________________________

Date Mailed: _____________________________

Tracking Number: _________________________

Date Received: ___________________________

Name: ___________________________________

Address: _________________________________

____

City, State, ZIP: __________________________

(Tape Receipt Here)

Gift Given & Amount: ______________________

Mailed Via: ______________________________

Date Mailed: _____________________________

Tracking Number: _________________________

Date Received: ___________________________

Name: ___________________________________

Address: _________________________________

____

City, State, ZIP: __________________________

(Tape Receipt Here)

Gift Given & Amount: ______________________

Mailed Via: ______________________________

Date Mailed: _____________________________

Tracking Number: _________________________

Date Received: ___________________________

Christmas Gift Tracker

Name: ___________________________________

Address: _________________________________

____

City, State, ZIP: ___________________________

(Tape Receipt Here)

Gift Given & Amount: ______________________

Mailed Via: _______________________________

Date Mailed: ______________________________

Tracking Number: _________________________

Date Received: ____________________________

Name: ___________________________________

Address: _________________________________

____

City, State, ZIP: ___________________________

(Tape Receipt Here)

Gift Given & Amount: ______________________

Mailed Via: _______________________________

Date Mailed: ______________________________

Tracking Number: _________________________

Date Received: ____________________________

Name: ___________________________________

Address: _________________________________

____

City, State, ZIP: ___________________________

(Tape Receipt Here)

Gift Given & Amount: ______________________

Mailed Via: _______________________________

Date Mailed: ______________________________

Tracking Number: _________________________

Date Received: ____________________________

Christmas Gift Tracker

Name: _______________________________
Address: _____________________________
____
City, State, ZIP: ______________________

Gift Given & Amount: __________________
Mailed Via: __________________________
Date Mailed: _________________________
Tracking Number: _____________________
Date Received: _______________________

(Tape Receipt Here)

Name: _______________________________
Address: _____________________________
____
City, State, ZIP: ______________________

Gift Given & Amount: __________________
Mailed Via: __________________________
Date Mailed: _________________________
Tracking Number: _____________________
Date Received: _______________________

(Tape Receipt Here)

Name: _______________________________
Address: _____________________________
____
City, State, ZIP: ______________________

Gift Given & Amount: __________________
Mailed Via: __________________________
Date Mailed: _________________________
Tracking Number: _____________________
Date Received: _______________________

(Tape Receipt Here)

Christmas Gift Tracker

Name: _______________________________
Address: _____________________________
____
City, State, ZIP: _____________________

(Tape Receipt Here)

Gift Given & Amount: _________________
Mailed Via: __________________________
Date Mailed: _________________________
Tracking Number: ____________________
Date Received: _______________________

Name: _______________________________
Address: _____________________________
____
City, State, ZIP: _____________________

(Tape Receipt Here)

Gift Given & Amount: _________________
Mailed Via: __________________________
Date Mailed: _________________________
Tracking Number: ____________________
Date Received: _______________________

Name: _______________________________
Address: _____________________________
____
City, State, ZIP: _____________________

(Tape Receipt Here)

Gift Given & Amount: _________________
Mailed Via: __________________________
Date Mailed: _________________________
Tracking Number: ____________________
Date Received: _______________________

Christmas Gift Tracker

Name: ______________________________
Address: ______________________________
____
City, State, ZIP: ______________________________

Gift Given & Amount: ______________________________
Mailed Via: ______________________________
Date Mailed: ______________________________
Tracking Number: ______________________________
Date Received: ______________________________

(Tape Receipt Here)

Name: ______________________________
Address: ______________________________
____
City, State, ZIP: ______________________________

Gift Given & Amount: ______________________________
Mailed Via: ______________________________
Date Mailed: ______________________________
Tracking Number: ______________________________
Date Received: ______________________________

(Tape Receipt Here)

Name: ______________________________
Address: ______________________________
____
City, State, ZIP: ______________________________

Gift Given & Amount: ______________________________
Mailed Via: ______________________________
Date Mailed: ______________________________
Tracking Number: ______________________________
Date Received: ______________________________

(Tape Receipt Here)

Christmas Gift Tracker

Name: _______________________________
Address: _______________________________
____
City, State, ZIP: _______________________________

(Tape Receipt Here)

Gift Given & Amount: _______________________
Mailed Via: _______________________________
Date Mailed: _______________________________
Tracking Number: _______________________
Date Received: _______________________________

Name: _______________________________
Address: _______________________________
____
City, State, ZIP: _______________________________

(Tape Receipt Here)

Gift Given & Amount: _______________________
Mailed Via: _______________________________
Date Mailed: _______________________________
Tracking Number: _______________________
Date Received: _______________________________

Name: _______________________________
Address: _______________________________
____
City, State, ZIP: _______________________________

(Tape Receipt Here)

Gift Given & Amount: _______________________
Mailed Via: _______________________________
Date Mailed: _______________________________
Tracking Number: _______________________
Date Received: _______________________________

Christmas Gift Tracker

Name: _______________________________
Address: _____________________________
____
City, State, ZIP: ______________________

Gift Given & Amount: __________________
Mailed Via: __________________________
Date Mailed: _________________________
Tracking Number: _____________________
Date Received: _______________________

(Tape Receipt Here)

Name: _______________________________
Address: _____________________________
____
City, State, ZIP: ______________________

Gift Given & Amount: __________________
Mailed Via: __________________________
Date Mailed: _________________________
Tracking Number: _____________________
Date Received: _______________________

(Tape Receipt Here)

Name: _______________________________
Address: _____________________________
____
City, State, ZIP: ______________________

Gift Given & Amount: __________________
Mailed Via: __________________________
Date Mailed: _________________________
Tracking Number: _____________________
Date Received: _______________________

(Tape Receipt Here)

Christmas Gift Tracker

Name: ___________________________
Address: _________________________
____
City, State, ZIP: ___________________

(Tape Receipt Here)

Gift Given & Amount: ________________
Mailed Via: _______________________
Date Mailed: ______________________
Tracking Number: ___________________
Date Received: _____________________

Name: ___________________________
Address: _________________________
____
City, State, ZIP: ___________________

(Tape Receipt Here)

Gift Given & Amount: ________________
Mailed Via: _______________________
Date Mailed: ______________________
Tracking Number: ___________________
Date Received: _____________________

Name: ___________________________
Address: _________________________
____
City, State, ZIP: ___________________

(Tape Receipt Here)

Gift Given & Amount: ________________
Mailed Via: _______________________
Date Mailed: ______________________
Tracking Number: ___________________
Date Received: _____________________

Christmas Gift Tracker

Name: _______________________________
Address: _____________________________
____
City, State, ZIP: ______________________

(Tape Receipt Here)

Gift Given & Amount: __________________
Mailed Via: ___________________________
Date Mailed: __________________________
Tracking Number: _____________________
Date Received: ________________________

Name: _______________________________
Address: _____________________________
____
City, State, ZIP: ______________________

(Tape Receipt Here)

Gift Given & Amount: __________________
Mailed Via: ___________________________
Date Mailed: __________________________
Tracking Number: _____________________
Date Received: ________________________

Name: _______________________________
Address: _____________________________
____
City, State, ZIP: ______________________

(Tape Receipt Here)

Gift Given & Amount: __________________
Mailed Via: ___________________________
Date Mailed: __________________________
Tracking Number: _____________________
Date Received: ________________________

Christmas Gift Tracker

Name: _______________________________
Address: _______________________________
____
City, State, ZIP: _______________________________

Gift Given & Amount: _______________________
Mailed Via: _______________________________
Date Mailed: _______________________________
Tracking Number: _______________________
Date Received: _______________________________

(Tape Receipt Here)

Name: _______________________________
Address: _______________________________
____
City, State, ZIP: _______________________________

Gift Given & Amount: _______________________
Mailed Via: _______________________________
Date Mailed: _______________________________
Tracking Number: _______________________
Date Received: _______________________________

(Tape Receipt Here)

Name: _______________________________
Address: _______________________________
____
City, State, ZIP: _______________________________

Gift Given & Amount: _______________________
Mailed Via: _______________________________
Date Mailed: _______________________________
Tracking Number: _______________________
Date Received: _______________________________

(Tape Receipt Here)

Christmas Gift Tracker

Name: _______________________________
Address: _____________________________
____
City, State, ZIP: ______________________

Gift Given & Amount: __________________
Mailed Via: ___________________________
Date Mailed: __________________________
Tracking Number: ______________________
Date Received: ________________________

(Tape Receipt Here)

Name: _______________________________
Address: _____________________________
____
City, State, ZIP: ______________________

Gift Given & Amount: __________________
Mailed Via: ___________________________
Date Mailed: __________________________
Tracking Number: ______________________
Date Received: ________________________

(Tape Receipt Here)

Name: _______________________________
Address: _____________________________
____
City, State, ZIP: ______________________

Gift Given & Amount: __________________
Mailed Via: ___________________________
Date Mailed: __________________________
Tracking Number: ______________________
Date Received: ________________________

(Tape Receipt Here)

Christmas Gift Tracker

Name: ___________________________________
Address: ________________________________
____
City, State, ZIP: _______________________

(Tape Receipt Here)

Gift Given & Amount: ____________________
Mailed Via: _____________________________
Date Mailed: ____________________________
Tracking Number: ________________________
Date Received: __________________________

Name: ___________________________________
Address: ________________________________
____
City, State, ZIP: _______________________

(Tape Receipt Here)

Gift Given & Amount: ____________________
Mailed Via: _____________________________
Date Mailed: ____________________________
Tracking Number: ________________________
Date Received: __________________________

Name: ___________________________________
Address: ________________________________
____
City, State, ZIP: _______________________

(Tape Receipt Here)

Gift Given & Amount: ____________________
Mailed Via: _____________________________
Date Mailed: ____________________________
Tracking Number: ________________________
Date Received: __________________________

Christmas Gift Tracker

Name: _______________________________
Address: _______________________________
____
City, State, ZIP: _______________________________

(Tape Receipt Here)

Gift Given & Amount: _______________________
Mailed Via: _______________________________
Date Mailed: _______________________________
Tracking Number: _______________________
Date Received: _______________________________

Name: _______________________________
Address: _______________________________
____
City, State, ZIP: _______________________________

(Tape Receipt Here)

Gift Given & Amount: _______________________
Mailed Via: _______________________________
Date Mailed: _______________________________
Tracking Number: _______________________
Date Received: _______________________________

Name: _______________________________
Address: _______________________________
____
City, State, ZIP: _______________________________

(Tape Receipt Here)

Gift Given & Amount: _______________________
Mailed Via: _______________________________
Date Mailed: _______________________________
Tracking Number: _______________________
Date Received: _______________________________

Christmas Gift Tracker

Name: _______________________________
Address: _______________________________
____
City, State, ZIP: _______________________________

(Tape Receipt Here)

Gift Given & Amount: _______________________
Mailed Via: _______________________________
Date Mailed: _______________________________
Tracking Number: _______________________
Date Received: _______________________________

Name: _______________________________
Address: _______________________________
____
City, State, ZIP: _______________________________

(Tape Receipt Here)

Gift Given & Amount: _______________________
Mailed Via: _______________________________
Date Mailed: _______________________________
Tracking Number: _______________________
Date Received: _______________________________

Name: _______________________________
Address: _______________________________
____
City, State, ZIP: _______________________________

(Tape Receipt Here)

Gift Given & Amount: _______________________
Mailed Via: _______________________________
Date Mailed: _______________________________
Tracking Number: _______________________
Date Received: _______________________________

Christmas Gift Tracker

Name: ___________________________________
Address: _________________________________
____
City, State, ZIP: __________________________

Gift Given & Amount: ____________________
Mailed Via: ______________________________
Date Mailed: _____________________________
Tracking Number: ________________________
Date Received: ___________________________

(Tape Receipt Here)

Name: ___________________________________
Address: _________________________________
____
City, State, ZIP: __________________________

Gift Given & Amount: ____________________
Mailed Via: ______________________________
Date Mailed: _____________________________
Tracking Number: ________________________
Date Received: ___________________________

(Tape Receipt Here)

Name: ___________________________________
Address: _________________________________
____
City, State, ZIP: __________________________

Gift Given & Amount: ____________________
Mailed Via: ______________________________
Date Mailed: _____________________________
Tracking Number: ________________________
Date Received: ___________________________

(Tape Receipt Here)

Christmas Gift Tracker

Name: _______________________________

Address: _____________________________

____

City, State, ZIP: _____________________

(Tape Receipt Here)

Gift Given & Amount: _________________

Mailed Via: __________________________

Date Mailed: _________________________

Tracking Number: ____________________

Date Received: _______________________

Name: _______________________________

Address: _____________________________

____

City, State, ZIP: _____________________

(Tape Receipt Here)

Gift Given & Amount: _________________

Mailed Via: __________________________

Date Mailed: _________________________

Tracking Number: ____________________

Date Received: _______________________

Name: _______________________________

Address: _____________________________

____

City, State, ZIP: _____________________

(Tape Receipt Here)

Gift Given & Amount: _________________

Mailed Via: __________________________

Date Mailed: _________________________

Tracking Number: ____________________

Date Received: _______________________

Christmas Gift Tracker

Name: _______________________________
Address: _______________________________
____
City, State, ZIP: _______________________________

(Tape Receipt Here)

Gift Given & Amount: _______________________
Mailed Via: _______________________________
Date Mailed: _______________________________
Tracking Number: _______________________
Date Received: _______________________________

Name: _______________________________
Address: _______________________________
____
City, State, ZIP: _______________________________

(Tape Receipt Here)

Gift Given & Amount: _______________________
Mailed Via: _______________________________
Date Mailed: _______________________________
Tracking Number: _______________________
Date Received: _______________________________

Name: _______________________________
Address: _______________________________
____
City, State, ZIP: _______________________________

(Tape Receipt Here)

Gift Given & Amount: _______________________
Mailed Via: _______________________________
Date Mailed: _______________________________
Tracking Number: _______________________
Date Received: _______________________________

Christmas Gift Tracker

Name: _______________________________

Address: _______________________________

____

City, State, ZIP: _______________________________

(Tape Receipt Here)

Gift Given & Amount: _______________________________

Mailed Via: _______________________________

Date Mailed: _______________________________

Tracking Number: _______________________________

Date Received: _______________________________

Name: _______________________________

Address: _______________________________

____

City, State, ZIP: _______________________________

(Tape Receipt Here)

Gift Given & Amount: _______________________________

Mailed Via: _______________________________

Date Mailed: _______________________________

Tracking Number: _______________________________

Date Received: _______________________________

Name: _______________________________

Address: _______________________________

____

City, State, ZIP: _______________________________

(Tape Receipt Here)

Gift Given & Amount: _______________________________

Mailed Via: _______________________________

Date Mailed: _______________________________

Tracking Number: _______________________________

Date Received: _______________________________

Christmas Gift Tracker

Name: _______________________________
Address: _____________________________
____
City, State, ZIP: _______________________

Gift Given & Amount: _________________
Mailed Via: ___________________________
Date Mailed: _________________________
Tracking Number: _____________________
Date Received: _______________________

(Tape Receipt Here)

Name: _______________________________
Address: _____________________________
____
City, State, ZIP: _______________________

Gift Given & Amount: _________________
Mailed Via: ___________________________
Date Mailed: _________________________
Tracking Number: _____________________
Date Received: _______________________

(Tape Receipt Here)

Name: _______________________________
Address: _____________________________
____
City, State, ZIP: _______________________

Gift Given & Amount: _________________
Mailed Via: ___________________________
Date Mailed: _________________________
Tracking Number: _____________________
Date Received: _______________________

(Tape Receipt Here)

Christmas Gift Tracker

Name: _______________________________
Address: _______________________________
____
City, State, ZIP: _______________________________

(Tape Receipt Here)

Gift Given & Amount: _______________________
Mailed Via: _______________________________
Date Mailed: _______________________________
Tracking Number: _______________________
Date Received: _______________________________

Name: _______________________________
Address: _______________________________
____
City, State, ZIP: _______________________________

(Tape Receipt Here)

Gift Given & Amount: _______________________
Mailed Via: _______________________________
Date Mailed: _______________________________
Tracking Number: _______________________
Date Received: _______________________________

Name: _______________________________
Address: _______________________________
____
City, State, ZIP: _______________________________

(Tape Receipt Here)

Gift Given & Amount: _______________________
Mailed Via: _______________________________
Date Mailed: _______________________________
Tracking Number: _______________________
Date Received: _______________________________

Christmas Gift Tracker

Name: _______________________________
Address: _______________________________
____
City, State, ZIP: _______________________________

Gift Given & Amount: _______________________________
Mailed Via: _______________________________
Date Mailed: _______________________________
Tracking Number: _______________________________
Date Received: _______________________________

(Tape Receipt Here)

Name: _______________________________
Address: _______________________________
____
City, State, ZIP: _______________________________

Gift Given & Amount: _______________________________
Mailed Via: _______________________________
Date Mailed: _______________________________
Tracking Number: _______________________________
Date Received: _______________________________

(Tape Receipt Here)

Name: _______________________________
Address: _______________________________
____
City, State, ZIP: _______________________________

Gift Given & Amount: _______________________________
Mailed Via: _______________________________
Date Mailed: _______________________________
Tracking Number: _______________________________
Date Received: _______________________________

(Tape Receipt Here)

Christmas Gift Tracker

Name: _______________________________

Address: _______________________________

____

City, State, ZIP: _______________________________

(Tape Receipt Here)

Gift Given & Amount: _______________________

Mailed Via: _______________________________

Date Mailed: _______________________________

Tracking Number: _______________________

Date Received: _______________________________

Name: _______________________________

Address: _______________________________

____

City, State, ZIP: _______________________________

(Tape Receipt Here)

Gift Given & Amount: _______________________

Mailed Via: _______________________________

Date Mailed: _______________________________

Tracking Number: _______________________

Date Received: _______________________________

Name: _______________________________

Address: _______________________________

____

City, State, ZIP: _______________________________

(Tape Receipt Here)

Gift Given & Amount: _______________________

Mailed Via: _______________________________

Date Mailed: _______________________________

Tracking Number: _______________________

Date Received: _______________________________

Christmas Gift Tracker

Name: _______________________________
Address: _______________________________
____
City, State, ZIP: _______________________________

Gift Given & Amount: _______________________
Mailed Via: _______________________________
Date Mailed: _______________________________
Tracking Number: _______________________
Date Received: _______________________________

(Tape Receipt Here)

Name: _______________________________
Address: _______________________________
____
City, State, ZIP: _______________________________

Gift Given & Amount: _______________________
Mailed Via: _______________________________
Date Mailed: _______________________________
Tracking Number: _______________________
Date Received: _______________________________

(Tape Receipt Here)

Name: _______________________________
Address: _______________________________
____
City, State, ZIP: _______________________________

Gift Given & Amount: _______________________
Mailed Via: _______________________________
Date Mailed: _______________________________
Tracking Number: _______________________
Date Received: _______________________________

(Tape Receipt Here)

Christmas Gift Tracker

Name: ________________________________
Address: ________________________________
____
City, State, ZIP: ________________________________

(Tape Receipt Here)

Gift Given & Amount: ________________________________
Mailed Via: ________________________________
Date Mailed: ________________________________
Tracking Number: ________________________________
Date Received: ________________________________

Name: ________________________________
Address: ________________________________
____
City, State, ZIP: ________________________________

(Tape Receipt Here)

Gift Given & Amount: ________________________________
Mailed Via: ________________________________
Date Mailed: ________________________________
Tracking Number: ________________________________
Date Received: ________________________________

Name: ________________________________
Address: ________________________________
____
City, State, ZIP: ________________________________

(Tape Receipt Here)

Gift Given & Amount: ________________________________
Mailed Via: ________________________________
Date Mailed: ________________________________
Tracking Number: ________________________________
Date Received: ________________________________

Christmas Gift Tracker

Name: _______________________________
Address: _______________________________
____
City, State, ZIP: _______________________________

Gift Given & Amount: _______________________
Mailed Via: _______________________________
Date Mailed: _______________________________
Tracking Number: _______________________
Date Received: _______________________

(Tape Receipt Here)

Name: _______________________________
Address: _______________________________
____
City, State, ZIP: _______________________________

Gift Given & Amount: _______________________
Mailed Via: _______________________________
Date Mailed: _______________________________
Tracking Number: _______________________
Date Received: _______________________

(Tape Receipt Here)

Name: _______________________________
Address: _______________________________
____
City, State, ZIP: _______________________________

Gift Given & Amount: _______________________
Mailed Via: _______________________________
Date Mailed: _______________________________
Tracking Number: _______________________
Date Received: _______________________

(Tape Receipt Here)

Christmas Gift Tracker

Name: ___________________________________
Address: ________________________________
____
City, State, ZIP: _______________________

(Tape Receipt Here)

Gift Given & Amount: ___________________
Mailed Via: ____________________________
Date Mailed: ___________________________
Tracking Number: _______________________
Date Received: _________________________

Name: ___________________________________
Address: ________________________________
____
City, State, ZIP: _______________________

(Tape Receipt Here)

Gift Given & Amount: ___________________
Mailed Via: ____________________________
Date Mailed: ___________________________
Tracking Number: _______________________
Date Received: _________________________

Name: ___________________________________
Address: ________________________________
____
City, State, ZIP: _______________________

(Tape Receipt Here)

Gift Given & Amount: ___________________
Mailed Via: ____________________________
Date Mailed: ___________________________
Tracking Number: _______________________
Date Received: _________________________

Christmas Gift Tracker

Name: _______________________________

Address: _____________________________

____

City, State, ZIP: _____________________

(Tape Receipt Here)

Gift Given & Amount: _________________

Mailed Via: __________________________

Date Mailed: _________________________

Tracking Number: _____________________

Date Received: _______________________

Name: _______________________________

Address: _____________________________

____

City, State, ZIP: _____________________

(Tape Receipt Here)

Gift Given & Amount: _________________

Mailed Via: __________________________

Date Mailed: _________________________

Tracking Number: _____________________

Date Received: _______________________

Name: _______________________________

Address: _____________________________

____

City, State, ZIP: _____________________

(Tape Receipt Here)

Gift Given & Amount: _________________

Mailed Via: __________________________

Date Mailed: _________________________

Tracking Number: _____________________

Date Received: _______________________

Christmas Gift Tracker

Name: ___________________________
Address: _________________________
____
City, State, ZIP: __________________

(Tape Receipt
Here)

Gift Given & Amount: ______________
Mailed Via: ______________________
Date Mailed: _____________________
Tracking Number: _________________
Date Received: ___________________

Name: ___________________________
Address: _________________________
____
City, State, ZIP: __________________

(Tape Receipt
Here)

Gift Given & Amount: ______________
Mailed Via: ______________________
Date Mailed: _____________________
Tracking Number: _________________
Date Received: ___________________

Name: ___________________________
Address: _________________________
____
City, State, ZIP: __________________

(Tape Receipt
Here)

Gift Given & Amount: ______________
Mailed Via: ______________________
Date Mailed: _____________________
Tracking Number: _________________
Date Received: ___________________

Christmas Gift Tracker

Name: ________________________________
Address: ________________________________
____
City, State, ZIP: ________________________________

(Tape Receipt Here)

Gift Given & Amount: ________________________
Mailed Via: ________________________________
Date Mailed: ________________________________
Tracking Number: ________________________
Date Received: ________________________________

Name: ________________________________
Address: ________________________________
____
City, State, ZIP: ________________________________

(Tape Receipt Here)

Gift Given & Amount: ________________________
Mailed Via: ________________________________
Date Mailed: ________________________________
Tracking Number: ________________________
Date Received: ________________________________

Name: ________________________________
Address: ________________________________
____
City, State, ZIP: ________________________________

(Tape Receipt Here)

Gift Given & Amount: ________________________
Mailed Via: ________________________________
Date Mailed: ________________________________
Tracking Number: ________________________
Date Received: ________________________________

Christmas Gift Tracker

Name: _________________________________
Address: _______________________________
____
City, State, ZIP: _______________________

(Tape Receipt Here)

Gift Given & Amount: ____________________
Mailed Via: _____________________________
Date Mailed: ____________________________
Tracking Number: _______________________
Date Received: __________________________

Name: _________________________________
Address: _______________________________
____
City, State, ZIP: _______________________

(Tape Receipt Here)

Gift Given & Amount: ____________________
Mailed Via: _____________________________
Date Mailed: ____________________________
Tracking Number: _______________________
Date Received: __________________________

Name: _________________________________
Address: _______________________________
____
City, State, ZIP: _______________________

(Tape Receipt Here)

Gift Given & Amount: ____________________
Mailed Via: _____________________________
Date Mailed: ____________________________
Tracking Number: _______________________
Date Received: __________________________

Christmas Gift Tracker

Name: _______________________________
Address: _______________________________
____
City, State, ZIP: _______________________________

(Tape Receipt Here)

Gift Given & Amount: _______________________
Mailed Via: _______________________________
Date Mailed: _______________________________
Tracking Number: _______________________
Date Received: _______________________

Name: _______________________________
Address: _______________________________
____
City, State, ZIP: _______________________________

(Tape Receipt Here)

Gift Given & Amount: _______________________
Mailed Via: _______________________________
Date Mailed: _______________________________
Tracking Number: _______________________
Date Received: _______________________

Name: _______________________________
Address: _______________________________
____
City, State, ZIP: _______________________________

(Tape Receipt Here)

Gift Given & Amount: _______________________
Mailed Via: _______________________________
Date Mailed: _______________________________
Tracking Number: _______________________
Date Received: _______________________

Christmas Gift Tracker

Name: _________________________________

Address: _______________________________

____

City, State, ZIP: _______________________

(Tape Receipt Here)

Gift Given & Amount: ___________________

Mailed Via: ____________________________

Date Mailed: ___________________________

Tracking Number: ______________________

Date Received: _________________________

Name: _________________________________

Address: _______________________________

____

City, State, ZIP: _______________________

(Tape Receipt Here)

Gift Given & Amount: ___________________

Mailed Via: ____________________________

Date Mailed: ___________________________

Tracking Number: ______________________

Date Received: _________________________

Name: _________________________________

Address: _______________________________

____

City, State, ZIP: _______________________

(Tape Receipt Here)

Gift Given & Amount: ___________________

Mailed Via: ____________________________

Date Mailed: ___________________________

Tracking Number: ______________________

Date Received: _________________________

Christmas Gift Tracker

Name: _______________________________
Address: _______________________________
____
City, State, ZIP: _______________________________

(Tape Receipt Here)

Gift Given & Amount: _______________________________
Mailed Via: _______________________________
Date Mailed: _______________________________
Tracking Number: _______________________________
Date Received: _______________________________

Name: _______________________________
Address: _______________________________
____
City, State, ZIP: _______________________________

(Tape Receipt Here)

Gift Given & Amount: _______________________________
Mailed Via: _______________________________
Date Mailed: _______________________________
Tracking Number: _______________________________
Date Received: _______________________________

Name: _______________________________
Address: _______________________________
____
City, State, ZIP: _______________________________

(Tape Receipt Here)

Gift Given & Amount: _______________________________
Mailed Via: _______________________________
Date Mailed: _______________________________
Tracking Number: _______________________________
Date Received: _______________________________

Christmas Gift Tracker

Name: _________________________________

Address: _______________________________

____

City, State, ZIP: _________________________

(Tape Receipt Here)

Gift Given & Amount: ____________________

Mailed Via: _____________________________

Date Mailed: ____________________________

Tracking Number: ________________________

Date Received: __________________________

Name: _________________________________

Address: _______________________________

____

City, State, ZIP: _________________________

(Tape Receipt Here)

Gift Given & Amount: ____________________

Mailed Via: _____________________________

Date Mailed: ____________________________

Tracking Number: ________________________

Date Received: __________________________

Name: _________________________________

Address: _______________________________

____

City, State, ZIP: _________________________

(Tape Receipt Here)

Gift Given & Amount: ____________________

Mailed Via: _____________________________

Date Mailed: ____________________________

Tracking Number: ________________________

Date Received: __________________________

Christmas Gift Tracker

Name: ________________________________

Address: ________________________________

____

City, State, ZIP: ________________________________

Gift Given & Amount: ________________________

Mailed Via: ________________________

Date Mailed: ________________________

Tracking Number: ________________________

Date Received: ________________________

(Tape Receipt Here)

Name: ________________________________

Address: ________________________________

____

City, State, ZIP: ________________________________

Gift Given & Amount: ________________________

Mailed Via: ________________________

Date Mailed: ________________________

Tracking Number: ________________________

Date Received: ________________________

(Tape Receipt Here)

Name: ________________________________

Address: ________________________________

____

City, State, ZIP: ________________________________

Gift Given & Amount: ________________________

Mailed Via: ________________________

Date Mailed: ________________________

Tracking Number: ________________________

Date Received: ________________________

(Tape Receipt Here)

Christmas Gift Tracker

Name: _______________________________

Address: _______________________________

____

City, State, ZIP: _______________________________

(Tape Receipt Here)

Gift Given & Amount: _______________________________

Mailed Via: _______________________________

Date Mailed: _______________________________

Tracking Number: _______________________________

Date Received: _______________________________

Name: _______________________________

Address: _______________________________

____

City, State, ZIP: _______________________________

(Tape Receipt Here)

Gift Given & Amount: _______________________________

Mailed Via: _______________________________

Date Mailed: _______________________________

Tracking Number: _______________________________

Date Received: _______________________________

Name: _______________________________

Address: _______________________________

____

City, State, ZIP: _______________________________

(Tape Receipt Here)

Gift Given & Amount: _______________________________

Mailed Via: _______________________________

Date Mailed: _______________________________

Tracking Number: _______________________________

Date Received: _______________________________

Christmas Gift Tracker

Name: _________________________________
Address: _______________________________
____
City, State, ZIP: _________________________

(Tape Receipt
Here)

Gift Given & Amount: ___________________
Mailed Via: ____________________________
Date Mailed: ___________________________
Tracking Number: _______________________
Date Received: _________________________

Name: _________________________________
Address: _______________________________
____
City, State, ZIP: _________________________

(Tape Receipt
Here)

Gift Given & Amount: ___________________
Mailed Via: ____________________________
Date Mailed: ___________________________
Tracking Number: _______________________
Date Received: _________________________

Name: _________________________________
Address: _______________________________
____
City, State, ZIP: _________________________

(Tape Receipt
Here)

Gift Given & Amount: ___________________
Mailed Via: ____________________________
Date Mailed: ___________________________
Tracking Number: _______________________
Date Received: _________________________

Christmas Gift Tracker

Name: _________________________________
Address: _________________________________
____
City, State, ZIP: _________________________________

(Tape Receipt Here)

Gift Given & Amount: _________________________
Mailed Via: _________________________________
Date Mailed: _________________________________
Tracking Number: _________________________
Date Received: _________________________________

Name: _________________________________
Address: _________________________________
____
City, State, ZIP: _________________________________

(Tape Receipt Here)

Gift Given & Amount: _________________________
Mailed Via: _________________________________
Date Mailed: _________________________________
Tracking Number: _________________________
Date Received: _________________________________

Name: _________________________________
Address: _________________________________
____
City, State, ZIP: _________________________________

(Tape Receipt Here)

Gift Given & Amount: _________________________
Mailed Via: _________________________________
Date Mailed: _________________________________
Tracking Number: _________________________
Date Received: _________________________________

Christmas Gift Tracker

Name: _______________________________

Address: _______________________________

____

City, State, ZIP: _______________________________

(Tape Receipt Here)

Gift Given & Amount: _______________________________

Mailed Via: _______________________________

Date Mailed: _______________________________

Tracking Number: _______________________________

Date Received: _______________________________

Name: _______________________________

Address: _______________________________

____

City, State, ZIP: _______________________________

(Tape Receipt Here)

Gift Given & Amount: _______________________________

Mailed Via: _______________________________

Date Mailed: _______________________________

Tracking Number: _______________________________

Date Received: _______________________________

Name: _______________________________

Address: _______________________________

____

City, State, ZIP: _______________________________

(Tape Receipt Here)

Gift Given & Amount: _______________________________

Mailed Via: _______________________________

Date Mailed: _______________________________

Tracking Number: _______________________________

Date Received: _______________________________

Christmas Gift Tracker

Name: _______________________________
Address: _____________________________
____
City, State, ZIP: _____________________

(Tape Receipt Here)

Gift Given & Amount: _________________
Mailed Via: __________________________
Date Mailed: _________________________
Tracking Number: _____________________
Date Received: _______________________

Name: _______________________________
Address: _____________________________
____
City, State, ZIP: _____________________

(Tape Receipt Here)

Gift Given & Amount: _________________
Mailed Via: __________________________
Date Mailed: _________________________
Tracking Number: _____________________
Date Received: _______________________

Name: _______________________________
Address: _____________________________
____
City, State, ZIP: _____________________

(Tape Receipt Here)

Gift Given & Amount: _________________
Mailed Via: __________________________
Date Mailed: _________________________
Tracking Number: _____________________
Date Received: _______________________

Christmas Gift Tracker

Name: _______________________________
Address: _______________________________
____
City, State, ZIP: _______________________________

(Tape Receipt
Here)

Gift Given & Amount: _______________________
Mailed Via: _______________________________
Date Mailed: _______________________________
Tracking Number: _______________________________
Date Received: _______________________________

Name: _______________________________
Address: _______________________________
____
City, State, ZIP: _______________________________

(Tape Receipt
Here)

Gift Given & Amount: _______________________
Mailed Via: _______________________________
Date Mailed: _______________________________
Tracking Number: _______________________________
Date Received: _______________________________

Name: _______________________________
Address: _______________________________
____
City, State, ZIP: _______________________________

(Tape Receipt
Here)

Gift Given & Amount: _______________________
Mailed Via: _______________________________
Date Mailed: _______________________________
Tracking Number: _______________________________
Date Received: _______________________________

Christmas Gift Tracker

Name: _______________________________
Address: _______________________________
____
City, State, ZIP: _______________________________

Gift Given & Amount: _______________________
Mailed Via: _______________________________
Date Mailed: _______________________________
Tracking Number: _______________________
Date Received: _______________________________

(Tape Receipt Here)

Name: _______________________________
Address: _______________________________
____
City, State, ZIP: _______________________________

Gift Given & Amount: _______________________
Mailed Via: _______________________________
Date Mailed: _______________________________
Tracking Number: _______________________
Date Received: _______________________________

(Tape Receipt Here)

Name: _______________________________
Address: _______________________________
____
City, State, ZIP: _______________________________

Gift Given & Amount: _______________________
Mailed Via: _______________________________
Date Mailed: _______________________________
Tracking Number: _______________________
Date Received: _______________________________

(Tape Receipt Here)

Christmas Gift Tracker

Name: _______________________________
Address: _____________________________
____
City, State, ZIP: _____________________

(Tape Receipt Here)

Gift Given & Amount: _________________
Mailed Via: __________________________
Date Mailed: _________________________
Tracking Number: _____________________
Date Received: _______________________

Name: _______________________________
Address: _____________________________
____
City, State, ZIP: _____________________

(Tape Receipt Here)

Gift Given & Amount: _________________
Mailed Via: __________________________
Date Mailed: _________________________
Tracking Number: _____________________
Date Received: _______________________

Name: _______________________________
Address: _____________________________
____
City, State, ZIP: _____________________

(Tape Receipt Here)

Gift Given & Amount: _________________
Mailed Via: __________________________
Date Mailed: _________________________
Tracking Number: _____________________
Date Received: _______________________

Christmas Gift Tracker

Name: ___________________________________

Address: _________________________________

____

City, State, ZIP: ___________________________

Gift Given & Amount: _______________________

Mailed Via: _______________________________

Date Mailed: ______________________________

Tracking Number: __________________________

Date Received: ____________________________

(Tape Receipt Here)

Name: ___________________________________

Address: _________________________________

____

City, State, ZIP: ___________________________

Gift Given & Amount: _______________________

Mailed Via: _______________________________

Date Mailed: ______________________________

Tracking Number: __________________________

Date Received: ____________________________

(Tape Receipt Here)

Name: ___________________________________

Address: _________________________________

____

City, State, ZIP: ___________________________

Gift Given & Amount: _______________________

Mailed Via: _______________________________

Date Mailed: ______________________________

Tracking Number: __________________________

Date Received: ____________________________

(Tape Receipt Here)

Christmas Gift Tracker

Name: _______________________________
Address: _______________________________
____
City, State, ZIP: _______________________________

(Tape Receipt Here)

Gift Given & Amount: _______________________________
Mailed Via: _______________________________
Date Mailed: _______________________________
Tracking Number: _______________________________
Date Received: _______________________________

Name: _______________________________
Address: _______________________________
____
City, State, ZIP: _______________________________

(Tape Receipt Here)

Gift Given & Amount: _______________________________
Mailed Via: _______________________________
Date Mailed: _______________________________
Tracking Number: _______________________________
Date Received: _______________________________

Name: _______________________________
Address: _______________________________
____
City, State, ZIP: _______________________________

(Tape Receipt Here)

Gift Given & Amount: _______________________________
Mailed Via: _______________________________
Date Mailed: _______________________________
Tracking Number: _______________________________
Date Received: _______________________________

Christmas Gift Tracker

Name: _______________________________
Address: _______________________________
____
City, State, ZIP: _______________________________

(Tape Receipt Here)

Gift Given & Amount: _______________________
Mailed Via: _______________________________
Date Mailed: _______________________________
Tracking Number: _______________________
Date Received: _______________________________

Name: _______________________________
Address: _______________________________
____
City, State, ZIP: _______________________________

(Tape Receipt Here)

Gift Given & Amount: _______________________
Mailed Via: _______________________________
Date Mailed: _______________________________
Tracking Number: _______________________
Date Received: _______________________________

Name: _______________________________
Address: _______________________________
____
City, State, ZIP: _______________________________

(Tape Receipt Here)

Gift Given & Amount: _______________________
Mailed Via: _______________________________
Date Mailed: _______________________________
Tracking Number: _______________________
Date Received: _______________________________

Christmas Gift Tracker

Name: ___________________________________
Address: _________________________________
____
City, State, ZIP: __________________________

(Tape Receipt Here)

Gift Given & Amount: _____________________
Mailed Via: ______________________________
Date Mailed: _____________________________
Tracking Number: ________________________
Date Received: ___________________________

Name: ___________________________________
Address: _________________________________
____
City, State, ZIP: __________________________

(Tape Receipt Here)

Gift Given & Amount: _____________________
Mailed Via: ______________________________
Date Mailed: _____________________________
Tracking Number: ________________________
Date Received: ___________________________

Name: ___________________________________
Address: _________________________________
____
City, State, ZIP: __________________________

(Tape Receipt Here)

Gift Given & Amount: _____________________
Mailed Via: ______________________________
Date Mailed: _____________________________
Tracking Number: ________________________
Date Received: ___________________________

Christmas Gift Tracker

Name: ____________________________________

Address: _________________________________

____

City, State, ZIP: ________________________

(Tape Receipt Here)

Gift Given & Amount: _____________________

Mailed Via: ______________________________

Date Mailed: _____________________________

Tracking Number: _________________________

Date Received: ___________________________

Name: ____________________________________

Address: _________________________________

____

City, State, ZIP: ________________________

(Tape Receipt Here)

Gift Given & Amount: _____________________

Mailed Via: ______________________________

Date Mailed: _____________________________

Tracking Number: _________________________

Date Received: ___________________________

Name: ____________________________________

Address: _________________________________

____

City, State, ZIP: ________________________

(Tape Receipt Here)

Gift Given & Amount: _____________________

Mailed Via: ______________________________

Date Mailed: _____________________________

Tracking Number: _________________________

Date Received: ___________________________

Christmas Gift Tracker

Name: ______________________________
Address: ____________________________
____
City, State, ZIP: _____________________

(Tape Receipt
Here)

Gift Given & Amount: _________________
Mailed Via: __________________________
Date Mailed: ________________________
Tracking Number: ____________________
Date Received: ______________________

Name: ______________________________
Address: ____________________________
____
City, State, ZIP: _____________________

(Tape Receipt
Here)

Gift Given & Amount: _________________
Mailed Via: __________________________
Date Mailed: ________________________
Tracking Number: ____________________
Date Received: ______________________

Name: ______________________________
Address: ____________________________
____
City, State, ZIP: _____________________

(Tape Receipt
Here)

Gift Given & Amount: _________________
Mailed Via: __________________________
Date Mailed: ________________________
Tracking Number: ____________________
Date Received: ______________________

Christmas Gift Tracker

Name: ________________________________
Address: ________________________________
____
City, State, ZIP: ________________________________

(Tape Receipt Here)

Gift Given & Amount: ________________________
Mailed Via: ________________________________
Date Mailed: ________________________________
Tracking Number: ______________________
Date Received: ________________________

Name: ________________________________
Address: ________________________________
____
City, State, ZIP: ________________________________

(Tape Receipt Here)

Gift Given & Amount: ________________________
Mailed Via: ________________________________
Date Mailed: ________________________________
Tracking Number: ______________________
Date Received: ________________________

Name: ________________________________
Address: ________________________________
____
City, State, ZIP: ________________________________

(Tape Receipt Here)

Gift Given & Amount: ________________________
Mailed Via: ________________________________
Date Mailed: ________________________________
Tracking Number: ______________________
Date Received: ________________________

Christmas Gift Tracker

Name: ___________________________________
Address: ________________________________
____
City, State, ZIP: _______________________

(Tape Receipt
Here)

Gift Given & Amount: ____________________
Mailed Via: _____________________________
Date Mailed: ____________________________
Tracking Number: ________________________
Date Received: __________________________

Name: ___________________________________
Address: ________________________________
____
City, State, ZIP: _______________________

(Tape Receipt
Here)

Gift Given & Amount: ____________________
Mailed Via: _____________________________
Date Mailed: ____________________________
Tracking Number: ________________________
Date Received: __________________________

Name: ___________________________________
Address: ________________________________
____
City, State, ZIP: _______________________

(Tape Receipt
Here)

Gift Given & Amount: ____________________
Mailed Via: _____________________________
Date Mailed: ____________________________
Tracking Number: ________________________
Date Received: __________________________

Christmas Gift Tracker

Name: ________________________________
Address: ______________________________
____
City, State, ZIP: _______________________

(Tape Receipt
Here)

Gift Given & Amount: __________________
Mailed Via: ___________________________
Date Mailed: __________________________
Tracking Number: _____________________
Date Received: ________________________

Name: ________________________________
Address: ______________________________
____
City, State, ZIP: _______________________

(Tape Receipt
Here)

Gift Given & Amount: __________________
Mailed Via: ___________________________
Date Mailed: __________________________
Tracking Number: _____________________
Date Received: ________________________

Name: ________________________________
Address: ______________________________
____
City, State, ZIP: _______________________

(Tape Receipt
Here)

Gift Given & Amount: __________________
Mailed Via: ___________________________
Date Mailed: __________________________
Tracking Number: _____________________
Date Received: ________________________

Christmas Gift Tracker

Name: _______________________________
Address: _____________________________
____
City, State, ZIP: _____________________

(Tape Receipt
Here)

Gift Given & Amount: _________________
Mailed Via: __________________________
Date Mailed: _________________________
Tracking Number: _____________________
Date Received: _______________________

Name: _______________________________
Address: _____________________________
____
City, State, ZIP: _____________________

(Tape Receipt
Here)

Gift Given & Amount: _________________
Mailed Via: __________________________
Date Mailed: _________________________
Tracking Number: _____________________
Date Received: _______________________

Name: _______________________________
Address: _____________________________
____
City, State, ZIP: _____________________

(Tape Receipt
Here)

Gift Given & Amount: _________________
Mailed Via: __________________________
Date Mailed: _________________________
Tracking Number: _____________________
Date Received: _______________________

Christmas Gift Tracker

Name: _________________________________
Address: _______________________________
____
City, State, ZIP: _________________________

(Tape Receipt Here)

Gift Given & Amount: ____________________
Mailed Via: _____________________________
Date Mailed: ____________________________
Tracking Number: _______________________
Date Received: __________________________

Name: _________________________________
Address: _______________________________
____
City, State, ZIP: _________________________

(Tape Receipt Here)

Gift Given & Amount: ____________________
Mailed Via: _____________________________
Date Mailed: ____________________________
Tracking Number: _______________________
Date Received: __________________________

Name: _________________________________
Address: _______________________________
____
City, State, ZIP: _________________________

(Tape Receipt Here)

Gift Given & Amount: ____________________
Mailed Via: _____________________________
Date Mailed: ____________________________
Tracking Number: _______________________
Date Received: __________________________

Christmas Gift Tracker

Name: _______________________________
Address: _____________________________
____
City, State, ZIP: _____________________

(Tape Receipt Here)

Gift Given & Amount: _________________
Mailed Via: __________________________
Date Mailed: _________________________
Tracking Number: _____________________
Date Received: _______________________

Name: _______________________________
Address: _____________________________
____
City, State, ZIP: _____________________

(Tape Receipt Here)

Gift Given & Amount: _________________
Mailed Via: __________________________
Date Mailed: _________________________
Tracking Number: _____________________
Date Received: _______________________

Name: _______________________________
Address: _____________________________
____
City, State, ZIP: _____________________

(Tape Receipt Here)

Gift Given & Amount: _________________
Mailed Via: __________________________
Date Mailed: _________________________
Tracking Number: _____________________
Date Received: _______________________

Christmas Gift Tracker

Name: ________________________________
Address: ________________________________
____
City, State, ZIP: ________________________________

Gift Given & Amount: ________________________
Mailed Via: ________________________________
Date Mailed: ________________________________
Tracking Number: ________________________
Date Received: ________________________________

(Tape Receipt Here)

Name: ________________________________
Address: ________________________________
____
City, State, ZIP: ________________________________

Gift Given & Amount: ________________________
Mailed Via: ________________________________
Date Mailed: ________________________________
Tracking Number: ________________________
Date Received: ________________________________

(Tape Receipt Here)

Name: ________________________________
Address: ________________________________
____
City, State, ZIP: ________________________________

Gift Given & Amount: ________________________
Mailed Via: ________________________________
Date Mailed: ________________________________
Tracking Number: ________________________
Date Received: ________________________________

(Tape Receipt Here)

Christmas Gift Tracker

Name: _______________________________
Address: _______________________________
____
City, State, ZIP: _______________________________

Gift Given & Amount: _______________________
Mailed Via: _______________________________
Date Mailed: _______________________________
Tracking Number: _______________________
Date Received: _______________________________

(Tape Receipt Here)

Name: _______________________________
Address: _______________________________
____
City, State, ZIP: _______________________________

Gift Given & Amount: _______________________
Mailed Via: _______________________________
Date Mailed: _______________________________
Tracking Number: _______________________
Date Received: _______________________________

(Tape Receipt Here)

Name: _______________________________
Address: _______________________________
____
City, State, ZIP: _______________________________

Gift Given & Amount: _______________________
Mailed Via: _______________________________
Date Mailed: _______________________________
Tracking Number: _______________________
Date Received: _______________________________

(Tape Receipt Here)

Christmas Gift Tracker

Name: _______________________________
Address: _______________________________
____
City, State, ZIP: _______________________________

(Tape Receipt Here)

Gift Given & Amount: _______________________________
Mailed Via: _______________________________
Date Mailed: _______________________________
Tracking Number: _______________________________
Date Received: _______________________________

Name: _______________________________
Address: _______________________________
____
City, State, ZIP: _______________________________

(Tape Receipt Here)

Gift Given & Amount: _______________________________
Mailed Via: _______________________________
Date Mailed: _______________________________
Tracking Number: _______________________________
Date Received: _______________________________

Name: _______________________________
Address: _______________________________
____
City, State, ZIP: _______________________________

(Tape Receipt Here)

Gift Given & Amount: _______________________________
Mailed Via: _______________________________
Date Mailed: _______________________________
Tracking Number: _______________________________
Date Received: _______________________________

Christmas Gift Tracker

Name: _______________________________
Address: _____________________________
____
City, State, ZIP: ______________________

(Tape Receipt
Here)

Gift Given & Amount: __________________
Mailed Via: ___________________________
Date Mailed: __________________________
Tracking Number: _____________________
Date Received: ________________________

Name: _______________________________
Address: _____________________________
____
City, State, ZIP: ______________________

(Tape Receipt
Here)

Gift Given & Amount: __________________
Mailed Via: ___________________________
Date Mailed: __________________________
Tracking Number: _____________________
Date Received: ________________________

Name: _______________________________
Address: _____________________________
____
City, State, ZIP: ______________________

(Tape Receipt
Here)

Gift Given & Amount: __________________
Mailed Via: ___________________________
Date Mailed: __________________________
Tracking Number: _____________________
Date Received: ________________________

Christmas Gift Tracker

Name: _______________________________
Address: _____________________________
____
City, State, ZIP: _______________________

(Tape Receipt Here)

Gift Given & Amount: __________________
Mailed Via: __________________________
Date Mailed: ________________________
Tracking Number: _____________________
Date Received: _______________________

Name: _______________________________
Address: _____________________________
____
City, State, ZIP: _______________________

(Tape Receipt Here)

Gift Given & Amount: __________________
Mailed Via: __________________________
Date Mailed: ________________________
Tracking Number: _____________________
Date Received: _______________________

Name: _______________________________
Address: _____________________________
____
City, State, ZIP: _______________________

(Tape Receipt Here)

Gift Given & Amount: __________________
Mailed Via: __________________________
Date Mailed: ________________________
Tracking Number: _____________________
Date Received: _______________________

Christmas Gift Tracker

Name: _______________________________
Address: _______________________________
____
City, State, ZIP: _______________________________

Gift Given & Amount: _______________________________
Mailed Via: _______________________________
Date Mailed: _______________________________
Tracking Number: _______________________________
Date Received: _______________________________

(Tape Receipt Here)

Name: _______________________________
Address: _______________________________
____
City, State, ZIP: _______________________________

Gift Given & Amount: _______________________________
Mailed Via: _______________________________
Date Mailed: _______________________________
Tracking Number: _______________________________
Date Received: _______________________________

(Tape Receipt Here)

Name: _______________________________
Address: _______________________________
____
City, State, ZIP: _______________________________

Gift Given & Amount: _______________________________
Mailed Via: _______________________________
Date Mailed: _______________________________
Tracking Number: _______________________________
Date Received: _______________________________

(Tape Receipt Here)

Christmas Gift Tracker

Name: _______________________________

Address: _______________________________

____

City, State, ZIP: _______________________________

(Tape Receipt Here)

Gift Given & Amount: _______________________________

Mailed Via: _______________________________

Date Mailed: _______________________________

Tracking Number: _______________________________

Date Received: _______________________________

Name: _______________________________

Address: _______________________________

____

City, State, ZIP: _______________________________

(Tape Receipt Here)

Gift Given & Amount: _______________________________

Mailed Via: _______________________________

Date Mailed: _______________________________

Tracking Number: _______________________________

Date Received: _______________________________

Name: _______________________________

Address: _______________________________

____

City, State, ZIP: _______________________________

(Tape Receipt Here)

Gift Given & Amount: _______________________________

Mailed Via: _______________________________

Date Mailed: _______________________________

Tracking Number: _______________________________

Date Received: _______________________________

Christmas Gift Tracker

Name: _______________________________
Address: _____________________________
____
City, State, ZIP: ____________________

(Tape Receipt Here)

Gift Given & Amount: _________________
Mailed Via: __________________________
Date Mailed: _________________________
Tracking Number: _____________________
Date Received: _______________________

Name: _______________________________
Address: _____________________________
____
City, State, ZIP: ____________________

(Tape Receipt Here)

Gift Given & Amount: _________________
Mailed Via: __________________________
Date Mailed: _________________________
Tracking Number: _____________________
Date Received: _______________________

Name: _______________________________
Address: _____________________________
____
City, State, ZIP: ____________________

(Tape Receipt Here)

Gift Given & Amount: _________________
Mailed Via: __________________________
Date Mailed: _________________________
Tracking Number: _____________________
Date Received: _______________________

Christmas Gift Tracker

Name: ___________________________
Address: _________________________
____
City, State, ZIP: ___________________

(Tape Receipt Here)

Gift Given & Amount: ________________
Mailed Via: _______________________
Date Mailed: ______________________
Tracking Number: __________________
Date Received: ____________________

Name: ___________________________
Address: _________________________
____
City, State, ZIP: ___________________

(Tape Receipt Here)

Gift Given & Amount: ________________
Mailed Via: _______________________
Date Mailed: ______________________
Tracking Number: __________________
Date Received: ____________________

Name: ___________________________
Address: _________________________
____
City, State, ZIP: ___________________

(Tape Receipt Here)

Gift Given & Amount: ________________
Mailed Via: _______________________
Date Mailed: ______________________
Tracking Number: __________________
Date Received: ____________________

Christmas Gift Tracker

Name: _________________________________
Address: _______________________________
____
City, State, ZIP: _______________________

(Tape Receipt Here)

Gift Given & Amount: ___________________
Mailed Via: ____________________________
Date Mailed: ___________________________
Tracking Number: _______________________
Date Received: _________________________

Name: _________________________________
Address: _______________________________
____
City, State, ZIP: _______________________

(Tape Receipt Here)

Gift Given & Amount: ___________________
Mailed Via: ____________________________
Date Mailed: ___________________________
Tracking Number: _______________________
Date Received: _________________________

Name: _________________________________
Address: _______________________________
____
City, State, ZIP: _______________________

(Tape Receipt Here)

Gift Given & Amount: ___________________
Mailed Via: ____________________________
Date Mailed: ___________________________
Tracking Number: _______________________
Date Received: _________________________

For Gifts
Received

Christmas Gift Tracker

Gift Received: __________________________
Received From: __________________________
Date Received: __________________________
Received Via: __________________________

Thank You Card Sent: O Yes O No   Date Mailed: [/   /   ]

Gift Received: __________________________
Received From: __________________________
Date Received: __________________________
Received Via: __________________________

Thank You Card Sent: O Yes O No   Date Mailed: [/   /   ]

Gift Received: __________________________
Received From: __________________________
Date Received: __________________________
Received Via: __________________________

Thank You Card Sent: O Yes O No   Date Mailed: [/   /   ]

Gift Received: __________________________
Received From: __________________________
Date Received: __________________________
Received Via: __________________________

Thank You Card Sent: O Yes O No   Date Mailed: [/   /   ]

Gift Received: __________________________
Received From: __________________________
Date Received: __________________________
Received Via: __________________________

Thank You Card Sent: O Yes O No   Date Mailed: [/   /   ]

Christmas Gift Tracker

Gift Received:
Received From:
Date Received:
Received Via:

Thank You Card Sent: O Yes O No   Date Mailed: [/ /]

Gift Received:
Received From:
Date Received:
Received Via:

Thank You Card Sent: O Yes O No   Date Mailed: [/ /]

Gift Received:
Received From:
Date Received:
Received Via:

Thank You Card Sent: O Yes O No   Date Mailed: [/ /]

Gift Received:
Received From:
Date Received:
Received Via:

Thank You Card Sent: O Yes O No   Date Mailed: [/ /]

Gift Received:
Received From:
Date Received:
Received Via:

Thank You Card Sent: O Yes O No   Date Mailed: [/ /]

Christmas Gift Tracker

Gift Received:
Received From:
Date Received:
Received Via:

Thank You Card Sent: O Yes O No   Date Mailed: [/ /]

Gift Received:
Received From:
Date Received:
Received Via:

Thank You Card Sent: O Yes O No   Date Mailed: [/ /]

Gift Received:
Received From:
Date Received:
Received Via:

Thank You Card Sent: O Yes O No   Date Mailed: [/ /]

Gift Received:
Received From:
Date Received:
Received Via:

Thank You Card Sent: O Yes O No   Date Mailed: [/ /]

Gift Received:
Received From:
Date Received:
Received Via:

Thank You Card Sent: O Yes O No   Date Mailed: [/ /]

Christmas Gift Tracker

Gift Received: ___________________________
Received From: ___________________________
Date Received: ___________________________
Received Via: ___________________________

Thank You Card Sent: O Yes O No   Date Mailed: [/ /]

Gift Received: ___________________________
Received From: ___________________________
Date Received: ___________________________
Received Via: ___________________________

Thank You Card Sent: O Yes O No   Date Mailed: [/ /]

Gift Received: ___________________________
Received From: ___________________________
Date Received: ___________________________
Received Via: ___________________________

Thank You Card Sent: O Yes O No   Date Mailed: [/ /]

Gift Received: ___________________________
Received From: ___________________________
Date Received: ___________________________
Received Via: ___________________________

Thank You Card Sent: O Yes O No   Date Mailed: [/ /]

Gift Received: ___________________________
Received From: ___________________________
Date Received: ___________________________
Received Via: ___________________________

Thank You Card Sent: O Yes O No   Date Mailed: [/ /]

Christmas Gift Tracker

Gift Received: ___________________________
Received From: ___________________________
Date Received: ___________________________
Received Via: ___________________________

Thank You Card Sent: ○ Yes ○ No   Date Mailed: [/   /   ]

Gift Received: ___________________________
Received From: ___________________________
Date Received: ___________________________
Received Via: ___________________________

Thank You Card Sent: ○ Yes ○ No   Date Mailed: [/   /   ]

Gift Received: ___________________________
Received From: ___________________________
Date Received: ___________________________
Received Via: ___________________________

Thank You Card Sent: ○ Yes ○ No   Date Mailed: [/   /   ]

Gift Received: ___________________________
Received From: ___________________________
Date Received: ___________________________
Received Via: ___________________________

Thank You Card Sent: ○ Yes ○ No   Date Mailed: [/   /   ]

Gift Received: ___________________________
Received From: ___________________________
Date Received: ___________________________
Received Via: ___________________________

Thank You Card Sent: ○ Yes ○ No   Date Mailed: [/   /   ]

Christmas Gift Tracker

Gift Received: ________________________________
Received From: ________________________________
Date Received: ________________________________
Received Via: ________________________________

Thank You Card Sent: O Yes O No Date Mailed: [/ /]

Gift Received: ________________________________
Received From: ________________________________
Date Received: ________________________________
Received Via: ________________________________

Thank You Card Sent: O Yes O No Date Mailed: [/ /]

Gift Received: ________________________________
Received From: ________________________________
Date Received: ________________________________
Received Via: ________________________________

Thank You Card Sent: O Yes O No Date Mailed: [/ /]

Gift Received: ________________________________
Received From: ________________________________
Date Received: ________________________________
Received Via: ________________________________

Thank You Card Sent: O Yes O No Date Mailed: [/ /]

Gift Received: ________________________________
Received From: ________________________________
Date Received: ________________________________
Received Via: ________________________________

Thank You Card Sent: O Yes O No Date Mailed: [/ /]

Christmas Gift Tracker

Gift Received: _______________________________

Received From: _______________________________

Date Received: _______________________________

Received Via: _______________________________

Thank You Card Sent: O Yes O No   Date Mailed: [/   /   ]

Gift Received: _______________________________

Received From: _______________________________

Date Received: _______________________________

Received Via: _______________________________

Thank You Card Sent: O Yes O No   Date Mailed: [/   /   ]

Gift Received: _______________________________

Received From: _______________________________

Date Received: _______________________________

Received Via: _______________________________

Thank You Card Sent: O Yes O No   Date Mailed: [/   /   ]

Gift Received: _______________________________

Received From: _______________________________

Date Received: _______________________________

Received Via: _______________________________

Thank You Card Sent: O Yes O No   Date Mailed: [/   /   ]

Gift Received: _______________________________

Received From: _______________________________

Date Received: _______________________________

Received Via: _______________________________

Thank You Card Sent: O Yes O No   Date Mailed: [/   /   ]

Christmas Gift Tracker

Gift Received: _______________________
Received From: _______________________
Date Received: _______________________
Received Via: _______________________

Thank You Card Sent: O Yes O No   Date Mailed: [/   /   ]

Gift Received: _______________________
Received From: _______________________
Date Received: _______________________
Received Via: _______________________

Thank You Card Sent: O Yes O No   Date Mailed: [/   /   ]

Gift Received: _______________________
Received From: _______________________
Date Received: _______________________
Received Via: _______________________

Thank You Card Sent: O Yes O No   Date Mailed: [/   /   ]

Gift Received: _______________________
Received From: _______________________
Date Received: _______________________
Received Via: _______________________

Thank You Card Sent: O Yes O No   Date Mailed: [/   /   ]

Gift Received: _______________________
Received From: _______________________
Date Received: _______________________
Received Via: _______________________

Thank You Card Sent: O Yes O No   Date Mailed: [/   /   ]

Christmas Gift Tracker

Gift Received: ___________________________
Received From: ___________________________
Date Received: ___________________________
Received Via: ___________________________

Thank You Card Sent: ○ Yes ○ No   Date Mailed: | / / |

Gift Received: ___________________________
Received From: ___________________________
Date Received: ___________________________
Received Via: ___________________________

Thank You Card Sent: ○ Yes ○ No   Date Mailed: | / / |

Gift Received: ___________________________
Received From: ___________________________
Date Received: ___________________________
Received Via: ___________________________

Thank You Card Sent: ○ Yes ○ No   Date Mailed: | / / |

Gift Received: ___________________________
Received From: ___________________________
Date Received: ___________________________
Received Via: ___________________________

Thank You Card Sent: ○ Yes ○ No   Date Mailed: | / / |

Gift Received: ___________________________
Received From: ___________________________
Date Received: ___________________________
Received Via: ___________________________

Thank You Card Sent: ○ Yes ○ No   Date Mailed: | / / |

Christmas Gift Tracker

Gift Received: ___________________________
Received From: ___________________________
Date Received: ___________________________
Received Via: ___________________________

Thank You Card Sent: O Yes O No   Date Mailed: [/   /   ]

Gift Received: ___________________________
Received From: ___________________________
Date Received: ___________________________
Received Via: ___________________________

Thank You Card Sent: O Yes O No   Date Mailed: [/   /   ]

Gift Received: ___________________________
Received From: ___________________________
Date Received: ___________________________
Received Via: ___________________________

Thank You Card Sent: O Yes O No   Date Mailed: [/   /   ]

Gift Received: ___________________________
Received From: ___________________________
Date Received: ___________________________
Received Via: ___________________________

Thank You Card Sent: O Yes O No   Date Mailed: [/   /   ]

Gift Received: ___________________________
Received From: ___________________________
Date Received: ___________________________
Received Via: ___________________________

Thank You Card Sent: O Yes O No   Date Mailed: [/   /   ]

Christmas Gift Tracker

Gift Received: ___________________________
Received From: ___________________________
Date Received: ___________________________
Received Via: ___________________________

Thank You Card Sent: O Yes O No   Date Mailed: [/ /]

Gift Received: ___________________________
Received From: ___________________________
Date Received: ___________________________
Received Via: ___________________________

Thank You Card Sent: O Yes O No   Date Mailed: [/ /]

Gift Received: ___________________________
Received From: ___________________________
Date Received: ___________________________
Received Via: ___________________________

Thank You Card Sent: O Yes O No   Date Mailed: [/ /]

Gift Received: ___________________________
Received From: ___________________________
Date Received: ___________________________
Received Via: ___________________________

Thank You Card Sent: O Yes O No   Date Mailed: [/ /]

Gift Received: ___________________________
Received From: ___________________________
Date Received: ___________________________
Received Via: ___________________________

Thank You Card Sent: O Yes O No   Date Mailed: [/ /]

Christmas Gift Tracker

Gift Received: _______________________

Received From: _______________________

Date Received: _______________________

Received Via: _______________________

Thank You Card Sent: O Yes O No   Date Mailed: [/   /   ]

Gift Received: _______________________

Received From: _______________________

Date Received: _______________________

Received Via: _______________________

Thank You Card Sent: O Yes O No   Date Mailed: [/   /   ]

Gift Received: _______________________

Received From: _______________________

Date Received: _______________________

Received Via: _______________________

Thank You Card Sent: O Yes O No   Date Mailed: [/   /   ]

Gift Received: _______________________

Received From: _______________________

Date Received: _______________________

Received Via: _______________________

Thank You Card Sent: O Yes O No   Date Mailed: [/   /   ]

Gift Received: _______________________

Received From: _______________________

Date Received: _______________________

Received Via: _______________________

Thank You Card Sent: O Yes O No   Date Mailed: [/   /   ]

Christmas Gift Tracker

Gift Received: _______________________________

Received From: _______________________________

Date Received: _______________________________

Received Via: _______________________________

Thank You Card Sent: O Yes O No Date Mailed: [/ /]

Gift Received: _______________________________

Received From: _______________________________

Date Received: _______________________________

Received Via: _______________________________

Thank You Card Sent: O Yes O No Date Mailed: [/ /]

Gift Received: _______________________________

Received From: _______________________________

Date Received: _______________________________

Received Via: _______________________________

Thank You Card Sent: O Yes O No Date Mailed: [/ /]

Gift Received: _______________________________

Received From: _______________________________

Date Received: _______________________________

Received Via: _______________________________

Thank You Card Sent: O Yes O No Date Mailed: [/ /]

Gift Received: _______________________________

Received From: _______________________________

Date Received: _______________________________

Received Via: _______________________________

Thank You Card Sent: O Yes O No Date Mailed: [/ /]

Christmas Gift Tracker

Gift Received: ___________________________________
Received From: ___________________________________
Date Received: ___________________________________
Received Via: ___________________________________

Thank You Card Sent: O Yes O No   Date Mailed: [/   /   ]

Gift Received: ___________________________________
Received From: ___________________________________
Date Received: ___________________________________
Received Via: ___________________________________

Thank You Card Sent: O Yes O No   Date Mailed: [/   /   ]

Gift Received: ___________________________________
Received From: ___________________________________
Date Received: ___________________________________
Received Via: ___________________________________

Thank You Card Sent: O Yes O No   Date Mailed: [/   /   ]

Gift Received: ___________________________________
Received From: ___________________________________
Date Received: ___________________________________
Received Via: ___________________________________

Thank You Card Sent: O Yes O No   Date Mailed: [/   /   ]

Gift Received: ___________________________________
Received From: ___________________________________
Date Received: ___________________________________
Received Via: ___________________________________

Thank You Card Sent: O Yes O No   Date Mailed: [/   /   ]

Christmas Gift Tracker

Gift Received: _______________________________
Received From: _______________________________
Date Received: _______________________________
Received Via: _______________________________

Thank You Card Sent: O Yes O No   Date Mailed: [/ /]

Gift Received: _______________________________
Received From: _______________________________
Date Received: _______________________________
Received Via: _______________________________

Thank You Card Sent: O Yes O No   Date Mailed: [/ /]

Gift Received: _______________________________
Received From: _______________________________
Date Received: _______________________________
Received Via: _______________________________

Thank You Card Sent: O Yes O No   Date Mailed: [/ /]

Gift Received: _______________________________
Received From: _______________________________
Date Received: _______________________________
Received Via: _______________________________

Thank You Card Sent: O Yes O No   Date Mailed: [/ /]

Gift Received: _______________________________
Received From: _______________________________
Date Received: _______________________________
Received Via: _______________________________

Thank You Card Sent: O Yes O No   Date Mailed: [/ /]

Christmas Gift Tracker

Gift Received: ____________________________
Received From: ____________________________
Date Received: ____________________________
Received Via: ____________________________

Thank You Card Sent: O Yes O No   Date Mailed: [/   /   ]

Gift Received: ____________________________
Received From: ____________________________
Date Received: ____________________________
Received Via: ____________________________

Thank You Card Sent: O Yes O No   Date Mailed: [/   /   ]

Gift Received: ____________________________
Received From: ____________________________
Date Received: ____________________________
Received Via: ____________________________

Thank You Card Sent: O Yes O No   Date Mailed: [/   /   ]

Gift Received: ____________________________
Received From: ____________________________
Date Received: ____________________________
Received Via: ____________________________

Thank You Card Sent: O Yes O No   Date Mailed: [/   /   ]

Gift Received: ____________________________
Received From: ____________________________
Date Received: ____________________________
Received Via: ____________________________

Thank You Card Sent: O Yes O No   Date Mailed: [/   /   ]

Christmas Gift Tracker

Gift Received: ______________________________

Received From: ______________________________

Date Received: ______________________________

Received Via: ______________________________

Thank You Card Sent: O Yes O No   Date Mailed: [/   /   ]

Gift Received: ______________________________

Received From: ______________________________

Date Received: ______________________________

Received Via: ______________________________

Thank You Card Sent: O Yes O No   Date Mailed: [/   /   ]

Gift Received: ______________________________

Received From: ______________________________

Date Received: ______________________________

Received Via: ______________________________

Thank You Card Sent: O Yes O No   Date Mailed: [/   /   ]

Gift Received: ______________________________

Received From: ______________________________

Date Received: ______________________________

Received Via: ______________________________

Thank You Card Sent: O Yes O No   Date Mailed: [/   /   ]

Gift Received: ______________________________

Received From: ______________________________

Date Received: ______________________________

Received Via: ______________________________

Thank You Card Sent: O Yes O No   Date Mailed: [/   /   ]

Christmas Gift Tracker

Gift Received: _______________________________
Received From: _______________________________
Date Received: _______________________________
Received Via: _______________________________

Thank You Card Sent: O Yes O No   Date Mailed: [/   /   ]

Gift Received: _______________________________
Received From: _______________________________
Date Received: _______________________________
Received Via: _______________________________

Thank You Card Sent: O Yes O No   Date Mailed: [/   /   ]

Gift Received: _______________________________
Received From: _______________________________
Date Received: _______________________________
Received Via: _______________________________

Thank You Card Sent: O Yes O No   Date Mailed: [/   /   ]

Gift Received: _______________________________
Received From: _______________________________
Date Received: _______________________________
Received Via: _______________________________

Thank You Card Sent: O Yes O No   Date Mailed: [/   /   ]

Gift Received: _______________________________
Received From: _______________________________
Date Received: _______________________________
Received Via: _______________________________

Thank You Card Sent: O Yes O No   Date Mailed: [/   /   ]

Christmas Gift Tracker

Gift Received: ___________________________
Received From: ___________________________
Date Received: ___________________________
Received Via: ___________________________

Thank You Card Sent: O Yes O No   Date Mailed: [/   /   ]

Gift Received: ___________________________
Received From: ___________________________
Date Received: ___________________________
Received Via: ___________________________

Thank You Card Sent: O Yes O No   Date Mailed: [/   /   ]

Gift Received: ___________________________
Received From: ___________________________
Date Received: ___________________________
Received Via: ___________________________

Thank You Card Sent: O Yes O No   Date Mailed: [/   /   ]

Gift Received: ___________________________
Received From: ___________________________
Date Received: ___________________________
Received Via: ___________________________

Thank You Card Sent: O Yes O No   Date Mailed: [/   /   ]

Gift Received: ___________________________
Received From: ___________________________
Date Received: ___________________________
Received Via: ___________________________

Thank You Card Sent: O Yes O No   Date Mailed: [/   /   ]

Christmas Gift Tracker

Gift Received: ______________________________

Received From: ______________________________

Date Received: ______________________________

Received Via: ______________________________

Thank You Card Sent: O Yes O No   Date Mailed: [/   /   ]

Gift Received: ______________________________

Received From: ______________________________

Date Received: ______________________________

Received Via: ______________________________

Thank You Card Sent: O Yes O No   Date Mailed: [/   /   ]

Gift Received: ______________________________

Received From: ______________________________

Date Received: ______________________________

Received Via: ______________________________

Thank You Card Sent: O Yes O No   Date Mailed: [/   /   ]

Gift Received: ______________________________

Received From: ______________________________

Date Received: ______________________________

Received Via: ______________________________

Thank You Card Sent: O Yes O No   Date Mailed: [/   /   ]

Gift Received: ______________________________

Received From: ______________________________

Date Received: ______________________________

Received Via: ______________________________

Thank You Card Sent: O Yes O No   Date Mailed: [/   /   ]

Christmas Gift Tracker

Gift Received: ____
Received From: ____
Date Received: ____
Received Via: ____

Thank You Card Sent: ◯ Yes ◯ No   Date Mailed: [/   /   ]

Gift Received: ____
Received From: ____
Date Received: ____
Received Via: ____

Thank You Card Sent: ◯ Yes ◯ No   Date Mailed: [/   /   ]

Gift Received: ____
Received From: ____
Date Received: ____
Received Via: ____

Thank You Card Sent: ◯ Yes ◯ No   Date Mailed: [/   /   ]

Gift Received: ____
Received From: ____
Date Received: ____
Received Via: ____

Thank You Card Sent: ◯ Yes ◯ No   Date Mailed: [/   /   ]

Gift Received: ____
Received From: ____
Date Received: ____
Received Via: ____

Thank You Card Sent: ◯ Yes ◯ No   Date Mailed: [/   /   ]

Christmas Gift Tracker

Gift Received: ___________________________
Received From: ___________________________
Date Received: ___________________________
Received Via: ___________________________

Thank You Card Sent: O Yes O No   Date Mailed: | / / |

Gift Received: ___________________________
Received From: ___________________________
Date Received: ___________________________
Received Via: ___________________________

Thank You Card Sent: O Yes O No   Date Mailed: | / / |

Gift Received: ___________________________
Received From: ___________________________
Date Received: ___________________________
Received Via: ___________________________

Thank You Card Sent: O Yes O No   Date Mailed: | / / |

Gift Received: ___________________________
Received From: ___________________________
Date Received: ___________________________
Received Via: ___________________________

Thank You Card Sent: O Yes O No   Date Mailed: | / / |

Gift Received: ___________________________
Received From: ___________________________
Date Received: ___________________________
Received Via: ___________________________

Thank You Card Sent: O Yes O No   Date Mailed: | / / |

Christmas Gift Tracker

Gift Received: _______________________________
Received From: _______________________________
Date Received: _______________________________
Received Via: _______________________________

Thank You Card Sent: O Yes O No   Date Mailed: [/ /]

Gift Received: _______________________________
Received From: _______________________________
Date Received: _______________________________
Received Via: _______________________________

Thank You Card Sent: O Yes O No   Date Mailed: [/ /]

Gift Received: _______________________________
Received From: _______________________________
Date Received: _______________________________
Received Via: _______________________________

Thank You Card Sent: O Yes O No   Date Mailed: [/ /]

Gift Received: _______________________________
Received From: _______________________________
Date Received: _______________________________
Received Via: _______________________________

Thank You Card Sent: O Yes O No   Date Mailed: [/ /]

Gift Received: _______________________________
Received From: _______________________________
Date Received: _______________________________
Received Via: _______________________________

Thank You Card Sent: O Yes O No   Date Mailed: [/ /]

Christmas Gift Tracker

Gift Received: ___________________________
Received From: ___________________________
Date Received: ___________________________
Received Via: ___________________________

Thank You Card Sent: O Yes O No   Date Mailed: [/   /   ]

Gift Received: ___________________________
Received From: ___________________________
Date Received: ___________________________
Received Via: ___________________________

Thank You Card Sent: O Yes O No   Date Mailed: [/   /   ]

Gift Received: ___________________________
Received From: ___________________________
Date Received: ___________________________
Received Via: ___________________________

Thank You Card Sent: O Yes O No   Date Mailed: [/   /   ]

Gift Received: ___________________________
Received From: ___________________________
Date Received: ___________________________
Received Via: ___________________________

Thank You Card Sent: O Yes O No   Date Mailed: [/   /   ]

Gift Received: ___________________________
Received From: ___________________________
Date Received: ___________________________
Received Via: ___________________________

Thank You Card Sent: O Yes O No   Date Mailed: [/   /   ]

Christmas Gift Tracker

Gift Received:
Received From:
Date Received:
Received Via:

Thank You Card Sent: O Yes O No   Date Mailed: [/   /   ]

Gift Received:
Received From:
Date Received:
Received Via:

Thank You Card Sent: O Yes O No   Date Mailed: [/   /   ]

Gift Received:
Received From:
Date Received:
Received Via:

Thank You Card Sent: O Yes O No   Date Mailed: [/   /   ]

Gift Received:
Received From:
Date Received:
Received Via:

Thank You Card Sent: O Yes O No   Date Mailed: [/   /   ]

Gift Received:
Received From:
Date Received:
Received Via:

Thank You Card Sent: O Yes O No   Date Mailed: [/   /   ]

Christmas Gift Tracker

Gift Received: _______________________________
Received From: _______________________________
Date Received: _______________________________
Received Via: _______________________________

Thank You Card Sent: O Yes O No   Date Mailed: [/ /]

Gift Received: _______________________________
Received From: _______________________________
Date Received: _______________________________
Received Via: _______________________________

Thank You Card Sent: O Yes O No   Date Mailed: [/ /]

Gift Received: _______________________________
Received From: _______________________________
Date Received: _______________________________
Received Via: _______________________________

Thank You Card Sent: O Yes O No   Date Mailed: [/ /]

Gift Received: _______________________________
Received From: _______________________________
Date Received: _______________________________
Received Via: _______________________________

Thank You Card Sent: O Yes O No   Date Mailed: [/ /]

Gift Received: _______________________________
Received From: _______________________________
Date Received: _______________________________
Received Via: _______________________________

Thank You Card Sent: O Yes O No   Date Mailed: [/ /]

Christmas Gift Tracker

Gift Received: _________________________________

Received From: _________________________________

Date Received: _________________________________

Received Via: _________________________________

Thank You Card Sent: O Yes O No   Date Mailed: [/   /   ]

Gift Received: _________________________________

Received From: _________________________________

Date Received: _________________________________

Received Via: _________________________________

Thank You Card Sent: O Yes O No   Date Mailed: [/   /   ]

Gift Received: _________________________________

Received From: _________________________________

Date Received: _________________________________

Received Via: _________________________________

Thank You Card Sent: O Yes O No   Date Mailed: [/   /   ]

Gift Received: _________________________________

Received From: _________________________________

Date Received: _________________________________

Received Via: _________________________________

Thank You Card Sent: O Yes O No   Date Mailed: [/   /   ]

Gift Received: _________________________________

Received From: _________________________________

Date Received: _________________________________

Received Via: _________________________________

Thank You Card Sent: O Yes O No   Date Mailed: [/   /   ]

Christmas Gift Tracker

Gift Received: ______________________________
Received From: ______________________________
Date Received: ______________________________
Received Via: ______________________________

Thank You Card Sent: O Yes O No   Date Mailed: | / / |

Gift Received: ______________________________
Received From: ______________________________
Date Received: ______________________________
Received Via: ______________________________

Thank You Card Sent: O Yes O No   Date Mailed: | / / |

Gift Received: ______________________________
Received From: ______________________________
Date Received: ______________________________
Received Via: ______________________________

Thank You Card Sent: O Yes O No   Date Mailed: | / / |

Gift Received: ______________________________
Received From: ______________________________
Date Received: ______________________________
Received Via: ______________________________

Thank You Card Sent: O Yes O No   Date Mailed: | / / |

Gift Received: ______________________________
Received From: ______________________________
Date Received: ______________________________
Received Via: ______________________________

Thank You Card Sent: O Yes O No Date Mailed: | / / |

Christmas Gift Tracker

Gift Received: ____
Received From: ____
Date Received: ____
Received Via: ____

Thank You Card Sent: O Yes O No   Date Mailed: [/   /   ]

Gift Received: ____
Received From: ____
Date Received: ____
Received Via: ____

Thank You Card Sent: O Yes O No   Date Mailed: [/   /   ]

Gift Received: ____
Received From: ____
Date Received: ____
Received Via: ____

Thank You Card Sent: O Yes O No   Date Mailed: [/   /   ]

Gift Received: ____
Received From: ____
Date Received: ____
Received Via: ____

Thank You Card Sent: O Yes O No   Date Mailed: [/   /   ]

Gift Received: ____
Received From: ____
Date Received: ____
Received Via: ____

Thank You Card Sent: O Yes O No Date Mailed: [/   /   ]

Christmas Gift Tracker

Gift Received: _______________________
Received From: _______________________
Date Received: _______________________
Received Via: _______________________

Thank You Card Sent: O Yes O No Date Mailed: [/ /]

Gift Received: _______________________
Received From: _______________________
Date Received: _______________________
Received Via: _______________________

Thank You Card Sent: O Yes O No Date Mailed: [/ /]

Gift Received: _______________________
Received From: _______________________
Date Received: _______________________
Received Via: _______________________

Thank You Card Sent: O Yes O No Date Mailed: [/ /]

Gift Received: _______________________
Received From: _______________________
Date Received: _______________________
Received Via: _______________________

Thank You Card Sent: O Yes O No Date Mailed: [/ /]

Gift Received: _______________________
Received From: _______________________
Date Received: _______________________
Received Via: _______________________

Thank You Card Sent: O Yes O No Date Mailed: [/ /]

Christmas Gift Tracker

Gift Received: _______________________________
Received From: _______________________________
Date Received: _______________________________
Received Via: _______________________________

Thank You Card Sent: O Yes O No   Date Mailed: [/   /   ]

Gift Received: _______________________________
Received From: _______________________________
Date Received: _______________________________
Received Via: _______________________________

Thank You Card Sent: O Yes O No   Date Mailed: [/   /   ]

Gift Received: _______________________________
Received From: _______________________________
Date Received: _______________________________
Received Via: _______________________________

Thank You Card Sent: O Yes O No   Date Mailed: [/   /   ]

Gift Received: _______________________________
Received From: _______________________________
Date Received: _______________________________
Received Via: _______________________________

Thank You Card Sent: O Yes O No   Date Mailed: [/   /   ]

Gift Received: _______________________________
Received From: _______________________________
Date Received: _______________________________
Received Via: _______________________________

Thank You Card Sent: O Yes O No   Date Mailed: [/   /   ]

Christmas Gift Tracker

Gift Received: ___________________________
Received From: ___________________________
Date Received: ___________________________
Received Via: ___________________________

Thank You Card Sent: O Yes O No   Date Mailed: [/   /   ]

Gift Received: ___________________________
Received From: ___________________________
Date Received: ___________________________
Received Via: ___________________________

Thank You Card Sent: O Yes O No   Date Mailed: [/   /   ]

Gift Received: ___________________________
Received From: ___________________________
Date Received: ___________________________
Received Via: ___________________________

Thank You Card Sent: O Yes O No   Date Mailed: [/   /   ]

Gift Received: ___________________________
Received From: ___________________________
Date Received: ___________________________
Received Via: ___________________________

Thank You Card Sent: O Yes O No   Date Mailed: [/   /   ]

Gift Received: ___________________________
Received From: ___________________________
Date Received: ___________________________
Received Via: ___________________________

Thank You Card Sent: O Yes O No   Date Mailed: [/   /   ]

Christmas Gift Tracker

Gift Received: ______________________________
Received From: ______________________________
Date Received: ______________________________
Received Via: ______________________________

Thank You Card Sent: O Yes O No   Date Mailed: [__ / __ / __]

Gift Received: ______________________________
Received From: ______________________________
Date Received: ______________________________
Received Via: ______________________________

Thank You Card Sent: O Yes O No   Date Mailed: [__ / __ / __]

Gift Received: ______________________________
Received From: ______________________________
Date Received: ______________________________
Received Via: ______________________________

Thank You Card Sent: O Yes O No   Date Mailed: [__ / __ / __]

Gift Received: ______________________________
Received From: ______________________________
Date Received: ______________________________
Received Via: ______________________________

Thank You Card Sent: O Yes O No   Date Mailed: [__ / __ / __]

Gift Received: ______________________________
Received From: ______________________________
Date Received: ______________________________
Received Via: ______________________________

Thank You Card Sent: O Yes O No   Date Mailed: [__ / __ / __]

Christmas Gift Tracker

Gift Received: ___________________________
Received From: ___________________________
Date Received: ___________________________
Received Via: ___________________________

Thank You Card Sent: O Yes O No   Date Mailed: [/ /]

Gift Received: ___________________________
Received From: ___________________________
Date Received: ___________________________
Received Via: ___________________________

Thank You Card Sent: O Yes O No   Date Mailed: [/ /]

Gift Received: ___________________________
Received From: ___________________________
Date Received: ___________________________
Received Via: ___________________________

Thank You Card Sent: O Yes O No   Date Mailed: [/ /]

Gift Received: ___________________________
Received From: ___________________________
Date Received: ___________________________
Received Via: ___________________________

Thank You Card Sent: O Yes O No   Date Mailed: [/ /]

Gift Received: ___________________________
Received From: ___________________________
Date Received: ___________________________
Received Via: ___________________________

Thank You Card Sent: O Yes O No   Date Mailed: [/ /]

Christmas Gift Tracker

Gift Received: _______________________________
Received From: _______________________________
Date Received: _______________________________
Received Via: _______________________________

Thank You Card Sent: O Yes O No   Date Mailed: [/   /   ]

Gift Received: _______________________________
Received From: _______________________________
Date Received: _______________________________
Received Via: _______________________________

Thank You Card Sent: O Yes O No   Date Mailed: [/   /   ]

Gift Received: _______________________________
Received From: _______________________________
Date Received: _______________________________
Received Via: _______________________________

Thank You Card Sent: O Yes O No   Date Mailed: [/   /   ]

Gift Received: _______________________________
Received From: _______________________________
Date Received: _______________________________
Received Via: _______________________________

Thank You Card Sent: O Yes O No   Date Mailed: [/   /   ]

Gift Received: _______________________________
Received From: _______________________________
Date Received: _______________________________
Received Via: _______________________________

Thank You Card Sent: O Yes O No   Date Mailed: [/   /   ]

Christmas Gift Tracker

Gift Received:
Received From:
Date Received:
Received Via:

Thank You Card Sent: O Yes O No   Date Mailed: [/   /   ]

Gift Received:
Received From:
Date Received:
Received Via:

Thank You Card Sent: O Yes O No   Date Mailed: [/   /   ]

Gift Received:
Received From:
Date Received:
Received Via:

Thank You Card Sent: O Yes O No   Date Mailed: [/   /   ]

Gift Received:
Received From:
Date Received:
Received Via:

Thank You Card Sent: O Yes O No   Date Mailed: [/   /   ]

Gift Received:
Received From:
Date Received:
Received Via:

Thank You Card Sent: O Yes O No   Date Mailed: [/   /   ]

Christmas Gift Tracker

Gift Received: _______________________________
Received From: _______________________________
Date Received: _______________________________
Received Via: _______________________________

Thank You Card Sent: O Yes O No   Date Mailed: [/ /]

Gift Received: _______________________________
Received From: _______________________________
Date Received: _______________________________
Received Via: _______________________________

Thank You Card Sent: O Yes O No   Date Mailed: [/ /]

Gift Received: _______________________________
Received From: _______________________________
Date Received: _______________________________
Received Via: _______________________________

Thank You Card Sent: O Yes O No   Date Mailed: [/ /]

Gift Received: _______________________________
Received From: _______________________________
Date Received: _______________________________
Received Via: _______________________________

Thank You Card Sent: O Yes O No   Date Mailed: [/ /]

Gift Received: _______________________________
Received From: _______________________________
Date Received: _______________________________
Received Via: _______________________________

Thank You Card Sent: O Yes O No   Date Mailed: [/ /]

Christmas Gift Tracker

Gift Received: ___________________________
Received From: ___________________________
Date Received: ___________________________
Received Via: ___________________________

Thank You Card Sent: O Yes O No   Date Mailed: [/ /]

Gift Received: ___________________________
Received From: ___________________________
Date Received: ___________________________
Received Via: ___________________________

Thank You Card Sent: O Yes O No   Date Mailed: [/ /]

Gift Received: ___________________________
Received From: ___________________________
Date Received: ___________________________
Received Via: ___________________________

Thank You Card Sent: O Yes O No   Date Mailed: [/ /]

Gift Received: ___________________________
Received From: ___________________________
Date Received: ___________________________
Received Via: ___________________________

Thank You Card Sent: O Yes O No   Date Mailed: [/ /]

Gift Received: ___________________________
Received From: ___________________________
Date Received: ___________________________
Received Via: ___________________________

Thank You Card Sent: O Yes O No   Date Mailed: [/ /]

Christmas Gift Tracker

Gift Received: ______________________________
Received From: ______________________________
Date Received: ______________________________
Received Via: ______________________________

Thank You Card Sent: O Yes O No Date Mailed: [/ /]

Gift Received: ______________________________
Received From: ______________________________
Date Received: ______________________________
Received Via: ______________________________

Thank You Card Sent: O Yes O No Date Mailed: [/ /]

Gift Received: ______________________________
Received From: ______________________________
Date Received: ______________________________
Received Via: ______________________________

Thank You Card Sent: O Yes O No Date Mailed: [/ /]

Gift Received: ______________________________
Received From: ______________________________
Date Received: ______________________________
Received Via: ______________________________

Thank You Card Sent: O Yes O No Date Mailed: [/ /]

Gift Received: ______________________________
Received From: ______________________________
Date Received: ______________________________
Received Via: ______________________________

Thank You Card Sent: O Yes O No Date Mailed: [/ /]

Christmas Gift Tracker

Gift Received: ______________________________
Received From: ______________________________
Date Received: ______________________________
Received Via: ______________________________

Thank You Card Sent: O Yes O No   Date Mailed: | / / |

Gift Received: ______________________________
Received From: ______________________________
Date Received: ______________________________
Received Via: ______________________________

Thank You Card Sent: O Yes O No   Date Mailed: | / / |

Gift Received: ______________________________
Received From: ______________________________
Date Received: ______________________________
Received Via: ______________________________

Thank You Card Sent: O Yes O No   Date Mailed: | / / |

Gift Received: ______________________________
Received From: ______________________________
Date Received: ______________________________
Received Via: ______________________________

Thank You Card Sent: O Yes O No   Date Mailed: | / / |

Gift Received: ______________________________
Received From: ______________________________
Date Received: ______________________________
Received Via: ______________________________

Thank You Card Sent: O Yes O No   Date Mailed: | / / |

Christmas Gift Tracker

Gift Received: _______________________________

Received From: _______________________________

Date Received: _______________________________

Received Via: _______________________________

Thank You Card Sent: O Yes O No   Date Mailed: [/   /   ]

Gift Received: _______________________________

Received From: _______________________________

Date Received: _______________________________

Received Via: _______________________________

Thank You Card Sent: O Yes O No   Date Mailed: [/   /   ]

Gift Received: _______________________________

Received From: _______________________________

Date Received: _______________________________

Received Via: _______________________________

Thank You Card Sent: O Yes O No   Date Mailed: [/   /   ]

Gift Received: _______________________________

Received From: _______________________________

Date Received: _______________________________

Received Via: _______________________________

Thank You Card Sent: O Yes O No   Date Mailed: [/   /   ]

Gift Received: _______________________________

Received From: _______________________________

Date Received: _______________________________

Received Via: _______________________________

Thank You Card Sent: O Yes O No   Date Mailed: [/   /   ]

Christmas Gift Tracker

Gift Received: _______________________________
Received From: _______________________________
Date Received: _______________________________
Received Via: _______________________________

Thank You Card Sent: O Yes O No   Date Mailed: [/ /]

Gift Received: _______________________________
Received From: _______________________________
Date Received: _______________________________
Received Via: _______________________________

Thank You Card Sent: O Yes O No   Date Mailed: [/ /]

Gift Received: _______________________________
Received From: _______________________________
Date Received: _______________________________
Received Via: _______________________________

Thank You Card Sent: O Yes O No   Date Mailed: [/ /]

Gift Received: _______________________________
Received From: _______________________________
Date Received: _______________________________
Received Via: _______________________________

Thank You Card Sent: O Yes O No   Date Mailed: [/ /]

Gift Received: _______________________________
Received From: _______________________________
Date Received: _______________________________
Received Via: _______________________________

Thank You Card Sent: O Yes O No   Date Mailed: [/ /]

Christmas Gift Tracker

Gift Received: _______________________________________
Received From: _______________________________________
Date Received: _______________________________________
Received Via: _______________________________________

Thank You Card Sent: O Yes O No   Date Mailed: [/   /   ]

Gift Received: _______________________________________
Received From: _______________________________________
Date Received: _______________________________________
Received Via: _______________________________________

Thank You Card Sent: O Yes O No   Date Mailed: [/   /   ]

Gift Received: _______________________________________
Received From: _______________________________________
Date Received: _______________________________________
Received Via: _______________________________________

Thank You Card Sent: O Yes O No   Date Mailed: [/   /   ]

Gift Received: _______________________________________
Received From: _______________________________________
Date Received: _______________________________________
Received Via: _______________________________________

Thank You Card Sent: O Yes O No   Date Mailed: [/   /   ]

Gift Received: _______________________________________
Received From: _______________________________________
Date Received: _______________________________________
Received Via: _______________________________________

Thank You Card Sent: O Yes O No   Date Mailed: [/   /   ]

Christmas Gift Tracker

Gift Received: ______________________________
Received From: ______________________________
Date Received: ______________________________
Received Via: ______________________________

Thank You Card Sent: ○ Yes ○ No   Date Mailed: | / / |

Gift Received: ______________________________
Received From: ______________________________
Date Received: ______________________________
Received Via: ______________________________

Thank You Card Sent: ○ Yes ○ No   Date Mailed: | / / |

Gift Received: ______________________________
Received From: ______________________________
Date Received: ______________________________
Received Via: ______________________________

Thank You Card Sent: ○ Yes ○ No   Date Mailed: | / / |

Gift Received: ______________________________
Received From: ______________________________
Date Received: ______________________________
Received Via: ______________________________

Thank You Card Sent: ○ Yes ○ No   Date Mailed: | / / |

Gift Received: ______________________________
Received From: ______________________________
Date Received: ______________________________
Received Via: ______________________________

Thank You Card Sent: ○ Yes ○ No   Date Mailed: | / / |

Christmas Gift Tracker

Gift Received: ___________________________
Received From: ___________________________
Date Received: ___________________________
Received Via: ___________________________

Thank You Card Sent: O Yes O No   Date Mailed: [/ /]

Gift Received: ___________________________
Received From: ___________________________
Date Received: ___________________________
Received Via: ___________________________

Thank You Card Sent: O Yes O No   Date Mailed: [/ /]

Gift Received: ___________________________
Received From: ___________________________
Date Received: ___________________________
Received Via: ___________________________

Thank You Card Sent: O Yes O No   Date Mailed: [/ /]

Gift Received: ___________________________
Received From: ___________________________
Date Received: ___________________________
Received Via: ___________________________

Thank You Card Sent: O Yes O No   Date Mailed: [/ /]

Gift Received: ___________________________
Received From: ___________________________
Date Received: ___________________________
Received Via: ___________________________

Thank You Card Sent: O Yes O No   Date Mailed: [/ /]

Christmas Gift Tracker

Gift Received: _______________________________________
Received From: _______________________________________
Date Received: _______________________________________
Received Via: _______________________________________

Thank You Card Sent: O Yes O No   Date Mailed: [/   /   ]

Gift Received: _______________________________________
Received From: _______________________________________
Date Received: _______________________________________
Received Via: _______________________________________

Thank You Card Sent: O Yes O No   Date Mailed: [/   /   ]

Gift Received: _______________________________________
Received From: _______________________________________
Date Received: _______________________________________
Received Via: _______________________________________

Thank You Card Sent: O Yes O No   Date Mailed: [/   /   ]

Gift Received: _______________________________________
Received From: _______________________________________
Date Received: _______________________________________
Received Via: _______________________________________

Thank You Card Sent: O Yes O No   Date Mailed: [/   /   ]

Gift Received: _______________________________________
Received From: _______________________________________
Date Received: _______________________________________
Received Via: _______________________________________

Thank You Card Sent: O Yes O No   Date Mailed: [/   /   ]

Christmas Gift Tracker

Gift Received: ______________________________
Received From: ______________________________
Date Received: ______________________________
Received Via: ______________________________

Thank You Card Sent: O Yes O No   Date Mailed: [/   /   ]

Gift Received: ______________________________
Received From: ______________________________
Date Received: ______________________________
Received Via: ______________________________

Thank You Card Sent: O Yes O No   Date Mailed: [/   /   ]

Gift Received: ______________________________
Received From: ______________________________
Date Received: ______________________________
Received Via: ______________________________

Thank You Card Sent: O Yes O No   Date Mailed: [/   /   ]

Gift Received: ______________________________
Received From: ______________________________
Date Received: ______________________________
Received Via: ______________________________

Thank You Card Sent: O Yes O No   Date Mailed: [/   /   ]

Gift Received: ______________________________
Received From: ______________________________
Date Received: ______________________________
Received Via: ______________________________

Thank You Card Sent: O Yes O No   Date Mailed: [/   /   ]

Christmas Gift Tracker

Gift Received:
Received From:
Date Received:
Received Via:

Thank You Card Sent: ⭕ Yes ⭕ No   Date Mailed: [/ /]

Gift Received:
Received From:
Date Received:
Received Via:

Thank You Card Sent: ⭕ Yes ⭕ No   Date Mailed: [/ /]

Gift Received:
Received From:
Date Received:
Received Via:

Thank You Card Sent: ⭕ Yes ⭕ No   Date Mailed: [/ /]

Gift Received:
Received From:
Date Received:
Received Via:

Thank You Card Sent: ⭕ Yes ⭕ No   Date Mailed: [/ /]

Gift Received:
Received From:
Date Received:
Received Via:

Thank You Card Sent: ⭕ Yes ⭕ No   Date Mailed: [/ /]

Christmas Gift Tracker

Gift Received: _______________________________
Received From: _______________________________
Date Received: _______________________________
Received Via: _______________________________

Thank You Card Sent: O Yes O No Date Mailed: [/   /   ]

Gift Received: _______________________________
Received From: _______________________________
Date Received: _______________________________
Received Via: _______________________________

Thank You Card Sent: O Yes O No Date Mailed: [/   /   ]

Gift Received: _______________________________
Received From: _______________________________
Date Received: _______________________________
Received Via: _______________________________

Thank You Card Sent: O Yes O No Date Mailed: [/   /   ]

Gift Received: _______________________________
Received From: _______________________________
Date Received: _______________________________
Received Via: _______________________________

Thank You Card Sent: O Yes O No Date Mailed: [/   /   ]

Gift Received: _______________________________
Received From: _______________________________
Date Received: _______________________________
Received Via: _______________________________

Thank You Card Sent: O Yes O No Date Mailed: [/   /   ]

Christmas Gift Tracker

Gift Received: ___________________________
Received From: ___________________________
Date Received: ___________________________
Received Via: ___________________________

Thank You Card Sent: O Yes O No   Date Mailed: [/ /]

Gift Received: ___________________________
Received From: ___________________________
Date Received: ___________________________
Received Via: ___________________________

Thank You Card Sent: O Yes O No   Date Mailed: [/ /]

Gift Received: ___________________________
Received From: ___________________________
Date Received: ___________________________
Received Via: ___________________________

Thank You Card Sent: O Yes O No   Date Mailed: [/ /]

Gift Received: ___________________________
Received From: ___________________________
Date Received: ___________________________
Received Via: ___________________________

Thank You Card Sent: O Yes O No   Date Mailed: [/ /]

Gift Received: ___________________________
Received From: ___________________________
Date Received: ___________________________
Received Via: ___________________________

Thank You Card Sent: O Yes O No   Date Mailed: [/ /]

Christmas Gift Tracker

Gift Received: ___________________________
Received From: ___________________________
Date Received: ___________________________
Received Via: ___________________________

Thank You Card Sent: O Yes O No   Date Mailed: [/ /]

Gift Received: ___________________________
Received From: ___________________________
Date Received: ___________________________
Received Via: ___________________________

Thank You Card Sent: O Yes O No   Date Mailed: [/ /]

Gift Received: ___________________________
Received From: ___________________________
Date Received: ___________________________
Received Via: ___________________________

Thank You Card Sent: O Yes O No   Date Mailed: [/ /]

Gift Received: ___________________________
Received From: ___________________________
Date Received: ___________________________
Received Via: ___________________________

Thank You Card Sent: O Yes O No   Date Mailed: [/ /]

Gift Received: ___________________________
Received From: ___________________________
Date Received: ___________________________
Received Via: ___________________________

Thank You Card Sent: O Yes O No   Date Mailed: [/ /]

Christmas Gift Tracker

Gift Received: ___________________________
Received From: ___________________________
Date Received: ___________________________
Received Via: ___________________________

Thank You Card Sent: O Yes O No   Date Mailed: [/   /   ]

Gift Received: ___________________________
Received From: ___________________________
Date Received: ___________________________
Received Via: ___________________________

Thank You Card Sent: O Yes O No   Date Mailed: [/   /   ]

Gift Received: ___________________________
Received From: ___________________________
Date Received: ___________________________
Received Via: ___________________________

Thank You Card Sent: O Yes O No   Date Mailed: [/   /   ]

Gift Received: ___________________________
Received From: ___________________________
Date Received: ___________________________
Received Via: ___________________________

Thank You Card Sent: O Yes O No   Date Mailed: [/   /   ]

Gift Received: ___________________________
Received From: ___________________________
Date Received: ___________________________
Received Via: ___________________________

Thank You Card Sent: O Yes O No   Date Mailed: [/   /   ]

Christmas Gift Tracker

Gift Received: ___________________________________
Received From: ___________________________________
Date Received: ___________________________________
Received Via: ___________________________________

Thank You Card Sent: O Yes O No   Date Mailed: [/   /   ]

Gift Received: ___________________________________
Received From: ___________________________________
Date Received: ___________________________________
Received Via: ___________________________________

Thank You Card Sent: O Yes O No   Date Mailed: [/   /   ]

Gift Received: ___________________________________
Received From: ___________________________________
Date Received: ___________________________________
Received Via: ___________________________________

Thank You Card Sent: O Yes O No   Date Mailed: [/   /   ]

Gift Received: ___________________________________
Received From: ___________________________________
Date Received: ___________________________________
Received Via: ___________________________________

Thank You Card Sent: O Yes O No   Date Mailed: [/   /   ]

Gift Received: ___________________________________
Received From: ___________________________________
Date Received: ___________________________________
Received Via: ___________________________________

Thank You Card Sent: O Yes O No   Date Mailed: [/   /   ]

Christmas Gift Tracker

Gift Received: ___________________________
Received From: ___________________________
Date Received: ___________________________
Received Via: ___________________________

Thank You Card Sent: O Yes O No   Date Mailed: [/   /   ]

Gift Received: ___________________________
Received From: ___________________________
Date Received: ___________________________
Received Via: ___________________________

Thank You Card Sent: O Yes O No   Date Mailed: [/   /   ]

Gift Received: ___________________________
Received From: ___________________________
Date Received: ___________________________
Received Via: ___________________________

Thank You Card Sent: O Yes O No   Date Mailed: [/   /   ]

Gift Received: ___________________________
Received From: ___________________________
Date Received: ___________________________
Received Via: ___________________________

Thank You Card Sent: O Yes O No   Date Mailed: [/   /   ]

Gift Received: ___________________________
Received From: ___________________________
Date Received: ___________________________
Received Via: ___________________________

Thank You Card Sent: O Yes O No   Date Mailed: [/   /   ]

Christmas Gift Tracker

Gift Received: _______________________________

Received From: _______________________________

Date Received: _______________________________

Received Via: _______________________________

Thank You Card Sent: O Yes O No   Date Mailed: [/   /   ]

Gift Received: _______________________________

Received From: _______________________________

Date Received: _______________________________

Received Via: _______________________________

Thank You Card Sent: O Yes O No   Date Mailed: [/   /   ]

Gift Received: _______________________________

Received From: _______________________________

Date Received: _______________________________

Received Via: _______________________________

Thank You Card Sent: O Yes O No   Date Mailed: [/   /   ]

Gift Received: _______________________________

Received From: _______________________________

Date Received: _______________________________

Received Via: _______________________________

Thank You Card Sent: O Yes O No   Date Mailed: [/   /   ]

Gift Received: _______________________________

Received From: _______________________________

Date Received: _______________________________

Received Via: _______________________________

Thank You Card Sent: O Yes O No   Date Mailed: [/   /   ]

Christmas Gift Tracker

Gift Received: ___________________________
Received From: ___________________________
Date Received: ___________________________
Received Via: ___________________________

Thank You Card Sent: O Yes O No Date Mailed: [/ /]

Gift Received: ___________________________
Received From: ___________________________
Date Received: ___________________________
Received Via: ___________________________

Thank You Card Sent: O Yes O No Date Mailed: [/ /]

Gift Received: ___________________________
Received From: ___________________________
Date Received: ___________________________
Received Via: ___________________________

Thank You Card Sent: O Yes O No Date Mailed: [/ /]

Gift Received: ___________________________
Received From: ___________________________
Date Received: ___________________________
Received Via: ___________________________

Thank You Card Sent: O Yes O No Date Mailed: [/ /]

Gift Received: ___________________________
Received From: ___________________________
Date Received: ___________________________
Received Via: ___________________________

Thank You Card Sent: O Yes O No Date Mailed: [/ /]

Christmas Gift Tracker

Gift Received:
Received From:
Date Received:
Received Via:

Thank You Card Sent: ○ Yes ○ No   Date Mailed: [/   /   ]

Gift Received:
Received From:
Date Received:
Received Via:

Thank You Card Sent: ○ Yes ○ No   Date Mailed: [/   /   ]

Gift Received:
Received From:
Date Received:
Received Via:

Thank You Card Sent: ○ Yes ○ No   Date Mailed: [/   /   ]

Gift Received:
Received From:
Date Received:
Received Via:

Thank You Card Sent: ○ Yes ○ No   Date Mailed: [/   /   ]

Gift Received:
Received From:
Date Received:
Received Via:

Thank You Card Sent: ○ Yes ○ No   Date Mailed: [/   /   ]

Christmas Gift Tracker

Gift Received: ___________________________
Received From: ___________________________
Date Received: ___________________________
Received Via: ___________________________

Thank You Card Sent: O Yes O No   Date Mailed: [/   /]

Gift Received: ___________________________
Received From: ___________________________
Date Received: ___________________________
Received Via: ___________________________

Thank You Card Sent: O Yes O No   Date Mailed: [/   /]

Gift Received: ___________________________
Received From: ___________________________
Date Received: ___________________________
Received Via: ___________________________

Thank You Card Sent: O Yes O No   Date Mailed: [/   /]

Gift Received: ___________________________
Received From: ___________________________
Date Received: ___________________________
Received Via: ___________________________

Thank You Card Sent: O Yes O No   Date Mailed: [/   /]

Gift Received: ___________________________
Received From: ___________________________
Date Received: ___________________________
Received Via: ___________________________

Thank You Card Sent: O Yes O No   Date Mailed: [/   /]

Christmas Gift Tracker

Gift Received: ___________________________
Received From: ___________________________
Date Received: ___________________________
Received Via: ___________________________

Thank You Card Sent: O Yes O No   Date Mailed: [/   /   ]

Gift Received: ___________________________
Received From: ___________________________
Date Received: ___________________________
Received Via: ___________________________

Thank You Card Sent: O Yes O No   Date Mailed: [/   /   ]

Gift Received: ___________________________
Received From: ___________________________
Date Received: ___________________________
Received Via: ___________________________

Thank You Card Sent: O Yes O No   Date Mailed: [/   /   ]

Gift Received: ___________________________
Received From: ___________________________
Date Received: ___________________________
Received Via: ___________________________

Thank You Card Sent: O Yes O No   Date Mailed: [/   /   ]

Gift Received: ___________________________
Received From: ___________________________
Date Received: ___________________________
Received Via: ___________________________

Thank You Card Sent: O Yes O No   Date Mailed: [/   /   ]

Christmas Gift Tracker

Gift Received: ______________________________
Received From: ______________________________
Date Received: ______________________________
Received Via: ______________________________

Thank You Card Sent: O Yes O No   Date Mailed: [/   /   ]

Gift Received: ______________________________
Received From: ______________________________
Date Received: ______________________________
Received Via: ______________________________

Thank You Card Sent: O Yes O No   Date Mailed: [/   /   ]

Gift Received: ______________________________
Received From: ______________________________
Date Received: ______________________________
Received Via: ______________________________

Thank You Card Sent: O Yes O No   Date Mailed: [/   /   ]

Gift Received: ______________________________
Received From: ______________________________
Date Received: ______________________________
Received Via: ______________________________

Thank You Card Sent: O Yes O No   Date Mailed: [/   /   ]

Gift Received: ______________________________
Received From: ______________________________
Date Received: ______________________________
Received Via: ______________________________

Thank You Card Sent: O Yes O No   Date Mailed: [/   /   ]

Christmas Gift Tracker

Gift Received: _______________________

Received From: _______________________

Date Received: _______________________

Received Via: _______________________

Thank You Card Sent: ○ Yes ○ No Date Mailed: [/   /   ]

Gift Received: _______________________

Received From: _______________________

Date Received: _______________________

Received Via: _______________________

Thank You Card Sent: ○ Yes ○ No Date Mailed: [/   /   ]

Gift Received: _______________________

Received From: _______________________

Date Received: _______________________

Received Via: _______________________

Thank You Card Sent: ○ Yes ○ No Date Mailed: [/   /   ]

Gift Received: _______________________

Received From: _______________________

Date Received: _______________________

Received Via: _______________________

Thank You Card Sent: ○ Yes ○ No Date Mailed: [/   /   ]

Gift Received: _______________________

Received From: _______________________

Date Received: _______________________

Received Via: _______________________

Thank You Card Sent: ○ Yes ○ No Date Mailed: [/   /   ]

Christmas Gift Tracker

Gift Received: _______________________________
Received From: _______________________________
Date Received: _______________________________
Received Via: _______________________________

Thank You Card Sent: O Yes O No   Date Mailed: [/   /   ]

Gift Received: _______________________________
Received From: _______________________________
Date Received: _______________________________
Received Via: _______________________________

Thank You Card Sent: O Yes O No   Date Mailed: [/   /   ]

Gift Received: _______________________________
Received From: _______________________________
Date Received: _______________________________
Received Via: _______________________________

Thank You Card Sent: O Yes O No   Date Mailed: [/   /   ]

Gift Received: _______________________________
Received From: _______________________________
Date Received: _______________________________
Received Via: _______________________________

Thank You Card Sent: O Yes O No   Date Mailed: [/   /   ]

Gift Received: _______________________________
Received From: _______________________________
Date Received: _______________________________
Received Via: _______________________________

Thank You Card Sent: O Yes O No   Date Mailed: [/   /   ]

Christmas Gift Tracker

Gift Received: _______________________
Received From: _______________________
Date Received: _______________________
Received Via: _______________________

Thank You Card Sent: O Yes O No   Date Mailed: [/   /   ]

Gift Received: _______________________
Received From: _______________________
Date Received: _______________________
Received Via: _______________________

Thank You Card Sent: O Yes O No   Date Mailed: [/   /   ]

Gift Received: _______________________
Received From: _______________________
Date Received: _______________________
Received Via: _______________________

Thank You Card Sent: O Yes O No   Date Mailed: [/   /   ]

Gift Received: _______________________
Received From: _______________________
Date Received: _______________________
Received Via: _______________________

Thank You Card Sent: O Yes O No   Date Mailed: [/   /   ]

Gift Received: _______________________
Received From: _______________________
Date Received: _______________________
Received Via: _______________________

Thank You Card Sent: O Yes O No   Date Mailed: [/   /   ]

Christmas Gift Tracker

Gift Received: _______________________________________
Received From: _______________________________________
Date Received: _______________________________________
Received Via: _______________________________________

Thank You Card Sent: O Yes O No   Date Mailed: [/ /]

Gift Received: _______________________________________
Received From: _______________________________________
Date Received: _______________________________________
Received Via: _______________________________________

Thank You Card Sent: O Yes O No   Date Mailed: [/ /]

Gift Received: _______________________________________
Received From: _______________________________________
Date Received: _______________________________________
Received Via: _______________________________________

Thank You Card Sent: O Yes O No   Date Mailed: [/ /]

Gift Received: _______________________________________
Received From: _______________________________________
Date Received: _______________________________________
Received Via: _______________________________________

Thank You Card Sent: O Yes O No   Date Mailed: [/ /]

Gift Received: _______________________________________
Received From: _______________________________________
Date Received: _______________________________________
Received Via: _______________________________________

Thank You Card Sent: O Yes O No   Date Mailed: [/ /]

Christmas Gift Tracker

Gift Received:
Received From:
Date Received:
Received Via:

Thank You Card Sent: O Yes O No   Date Mailed: ___ / ___ / ___

Gift Received:
Received From:
Date Received:
Received Via:

Thank You Card Sent: O Yes O No   Date Mailed: ___ / ___ / ___

Gift Received:
Received From:
Date Received:
Received Via:

Thank You Card Sent: O Yes O No   Date Mailed: ___ / ___ / ___

Gift Received:
Received From:
Date Received:
Received Via:

Thank You Card Sent: O Yes O No   Date Mailed: ___ / ___ / ___

Gift Received:
Received From:
Date Received:
Received Via:

Thank You Card Sent: O Yes O No   Date Mailed: ___ / ___ / ___

Christmas Gift Tracker

Gift Received: _______________________________
Received From: _______________________________
Date Received: _______________________________
Received Via: _______________________________

Thank You Card Sent: ○ Yes ○ No   Date Mailed: [/   /   ]

Gift Received: _______________________________
Received From: _______________________________
Date Received: _______________________________
Received Via: _______________________________

Thank You Card Sent: ○ Yes ○ No   Date Mailed: [/   /   ]

Gift Received: _______________________________
Received From: _______________________________
Date Received: _______________________________
Received Via: _______________________________

Thank You Card Sent: ○ Yes ○ No   Date Mailed: [/   /   ]

Gift Received: _______________________________
Received From: _______________________________
Date Received: _______________________________
Received Via: _______________________________

Thank You Card Sent: ○ Yes ○ No   Date Mailed: [/   /   ]

Gift Received: _______________________________
Received From: _______________________________
Date Received: _______________________________
Received Via: _______________________________

Thank You Card Sent: ○ Yes ○ No   Date Mailed: [/   /   ]

Christmas Gift Tracker

Gift Received: _______________________________________
Received From: _______________________________________
Date Received: _______________________________________
Received Via: _______________________________________

Thank You Card Sent: O Yes O No   Date Mailed: [/ /]

Gift Received: _______________________________________
Received From: _______________________________________
Date Received: _______________________________________
Received Via: _______________________________________

Thank You Card Sent: O Yes O No   Date Mailed: [/ /]

Gift Received: _______________________________________
Received From: _______________________________________
Date Received: _______________________________________
Received Via: _______________________________________

Thank You Card Sent: O Yes O No   Date Mailed: [/ /]

Gift Received: _______________________________________
Received From: _______________________________________
Date Received: _______________________________________
Received Via: _______________________________________

Thank You Card Sent: O Yes O No   Date Mailed: [/ /]

Gift Received: _______________________________________
Received From: _______________________________________
Date Received: _______________________________________
Received Via: _______________________________________

Thank You Card Sent: O Yes O No   Date Mailed: [/ /]

Christmas Gift Tracker

Gift Received: _______________________________
Received From: _______________________________
Date Received: _______________________________
Received Via: _______________________________

Thank You Card Sent: O Yes O No   Date Mailed: [/   /   ]

Gift Received: _______________________________
Received From: _______________________________
Date Received: _______________________________
Received Via: _______________________________

Thank You Card Sent: O Yes O No   Date Mailed: [/   /   ]

Gift Received: _______________________________
Received From: _______________________________
Date Received: _______________________________
Received Via: _______________________________

Thank You Card Sent: O Yes O No   Date Mailed: [/   /   ]

Gift Received: _______________________________
Received From: _______________________________
Date Received: _______________________________
Received Via: _______________________________

Thank You Card Sent: O Yes O No   Date Mailed: [/   /   ]

Gift Received: _______________________________
Received From: _______________________________
Date Received: _______________________________
Received Via: _______________________________

Thank You Card Sent: O Yes O No   Date Mailed: [/   /   ]

Christmas Gift Tracker

Gift Received: _______________________
Received From: _______________________
Date Received: _______________________
Received Via: _______________________

Thank You Card Sent: O Yes O No   Date Mailed: [/   /]

Gift Received: _______________________
Received From: _______________________
Date Received: _______________________
Received Via: _______________________

Thank You Card Sent: O Yes O No   Date Mailed: [/   /]

Gift Received: _______________________
Received From: _______________________
Date Received: _______________________
Received Via: _______________________

Thank You Card Sent: O Yes O No   Date Mailed: [/   /]

Gift Received: _______________________
Received From: _______________________
Date Received: _______________________
Received Via: _______________________

Thank You Card Sent: O Yes O No   Date Mailed: [/   /]

Gift Received: _______________________
Received From: _______________________
Date Received: _______________________
Received Via: _______________________

Thank You Card Sent: O Yes O No   Date Mailed: [/   /]

Christmas Gift Tracker

Gift Received: ______________________
Received From: ______________________
Date Received: ______________________
Received Via: ______________________

Thank You Card Sent: O Yes O No   Date Mailed: [/   /   ]

Gift Received: ______________________
Received From: ______________________
Date Received: ______________________
Received Via: ______________________

Thank You Card Sent: O Yes O No   Date Mailed: [/   /   ]

Gift Received: ______________________
Received From: ______________________
Date Received: ______________________
Received Via: ______________________

Thank You Card Sent: O Yes O No   Date Mailed: [/   /   ]

Gift Received: ______________________
Received From: ______________________
Date Received: ______________________
Received Via: ______________________

Thank You Card Sent: O Yes O No   Date Mailed: [/   /   ]

Gift Received: ______________________
Received From: ______________________
Date Received: ______________________
Received Via: ______________________

Thank You Card Sent: O Yes O No   Date Mailed: [/   /   ]

Christmas Gift Tracker

Gift Received: ___________________________
Received From: ___________________________
Date Received: ___________________________
Received Via: ___________________________

Thank You Card Sent: O Yes O No   Date Mailed: [/   /   ]

Gift Received: ___________________________
Received From: ___________________________
Date Received: ___________________________
Received Via: ___________________________

Thank You Card Sent: O Yes O No   Date Mailed: [/   /   ]

Gift Received: ___________________________
Received From: ___________________________
Date Received: ___________________________
Received Via: ___________________________

Thank You Card Sent: O Yes O No   Date Mailed: [/   /   ]

Gift Received: ___________________________
Received From: ___________________________
Date Received: ___________________________
Received Via: ___________________________

Thank You Card Sent: O Yes O No   Date Mailed: [/   /   ]

Gift Received: ___________________________
Received From: ___________________________
Date Received: ___________________________
Received Via: ___________________________

Thank You Card Sent: O Yes O No   Date Mailed: [/   /   ]

Christmas Gift Tracker

Gift Received: _______________________________
Received From: _______________________________
Date Received: _______________________________
Received Via: _______________________________

Thank You Card Sent: O Yes O No   Date Mailed: [/ /]

Gift Received: _______________________________
Received From: _______________________________
Date Received: _______________________________
Received Via: _______________________________

Thank You Card Sent: O Yes O No   Date Mailed: [/ /]

Gift Received: _______________________________
Received From: _______________________________
Date Received: _______________________________
Received Via: _______________________________

Thank You Card Sent: O Yes O No   Date Mailed: [/ /]

Gift Received: _______________________________
Received From: _______________________________
Date Received: _______________________________
Received Via: _______________________________

Thank You Card Sent: O Yes O No   Date Mailed: [/ /]

Gift Received: _______________________________
Received From: _______________________________
Date Received: _______________________________
Received Via: _______________________________

Thank You Card Sent: O Yes O No   Date Mailed: [/ /]

Christmas Gift Tracker

Gift Received: ______________________________
Received From: ______________________________
Date Received: ______________________________
Received Via: ______________________________

Thank You Card Sent: O Yes O No   Date Mailed: [/   /]

Gift Received: ______________________________
Received From: ______________________________
Date Received: ______________________________
Received Via: ______________________________

Thank You Card Sent: O Yes O No   Date Mailed: [/   /]

Gift Received: ______________________________
Received From: ______________________________
Date Received: ______________________________
Received Via: ______________________________

Thank You Card Sent: O Yes O No   Date Mailed: [/   /]

Gift Received: ______________________________
Received From: ______________________________
Date Received: ______________________________
Received Via: ______________________________

Thank You Card Sent: O Yes O No   Date Mailed: [/   /]

Gift Received: ______________________________
Received From: ______________________________
Date Received: ______________________________
Received Via: ______________________________

Thank You Card Sent: O Yes O No   Date Mailed: [/   /]

Christmas Gift Tracker

Gift Received: _______________________

Received From: _______________________

Date Received: _______________________

Received Via: _______________________

Thank You Card Sent: O Yes O No   Date Mailed: [/   /   ]

Gift Received: _______________________

Received From: _______________________

Date Received: _______________________

Received Via: _______________________

Thank You Card Sent: O Yes O No   Date Mailed: [/   /   ]

Gift Received: _______________________

Received From: _______________________

Date Received: _______________________

Received Via: _______________________

Thank You Card Sent: O Yes O No   Date Mailed: [/   /   ]

Gift Received: _______________________

Received From: _______________________

Date Received: _______________________

Received Via: _______________________

Thank You Card Sent: O Yes O No   Date Mailed: [/   /   ]

Gift Received: _______________________

Received From: _______________________

Date Received: _______________________

Received Via: _______________________

Thank You Card Sent: O Yes O No   Date Mailed: [/   /   ]

Christmas Gift Tracker

Gift Received: ___________________________
Received From: ___________________________
Date Received: ___________________________
Received Via: ___________________________

Thank You Card Sent: O Yes O No   Date Mailed: [/   /   ]

Gift Received: ___________________________
Received From: ___________________________
Date Received: ___________________________
Received Via: ___________________________

Thank You Card Sent: O Yes O No   Date Mailed: [/   /   ]

Gift Received: ___________________________
Received From: ___________________________
Date Received: ___________________________
Received Via: ___________________________

Thank You Card Sent: O Yes O No   Date Mailed: [/   /   ]

Gift Received: ___________________________
Received From: ___________________________
Date Received: ___________________________
Received Via: ___________________________

Thank You Card Sent: O Yes O No   Date Mailed: [/   /   ]

Gift Received: ___________________________
Received From: ___________________________
Date Received: ___________________________
Received Via: ___________________________

Thank You Card Sent: O Yes O No   Date Mailed: [/   /   ]

Christmas Gift Tracker

Gift Received: ___________________________
Received From: ___________________________
Date Received: ___________________________
Received Via: ___________________________

Thank You Card Sent: O Yes O No   Date Mailed: [/ /]

Gift Received: ___________________________
Received From: ___________________________
Date Received: ___________________________
Received Via: ___________________________

Thank You Card Sent: O Yes O No   Date Mailed: [/ /]

Gift Received: ___________________________
Received From: ___________________________
Date Received: ___________________________
Received Via: ___________________________

Thank You Card Sent: O Yes O No   Date Mailed: [/ /]

Gift Received: ___________________________
Received From: ___________________________
Date Received: ___________________________
Received Via: ___________________________

Thank You Card Sent: O Yes O No   Date Mailed: [/ /]

Gift Received: ___________________________
Received From: ___________________________
Date Received: ___________________________
Received Via: ___________________________

Thank You Card Sent: O Yes O No   Date Mailed: [/ /]

Christmas Gift Tracker

Gift Received: _______________________________
Received From: _______________________________
Date Received: _______________________________
Received Via: _______________________________

Thank You Card Sent: O Yes O No   Date Mailed: [/ /]

Gift Received: _______________________________
Received From: _______________________________
Date Received: _______________________________
Received Via: _______________________________

Thank You Card Sent: O Yes O No   Date Mailed: [/ /]

Gift Received: _______________________________
Received From: _______________________________
Date Received: _______________________________
Received Via: _______________________________

Thank You Card Sent: O Yes O No   Date Mailed: [/ /]

Gift Received: _______________________________
Received From: _______________________________
Date Received: _______________________________
Received Via: _______________________________

Thank You Card Sent: O Yes O No   Date Mailed: [/ /]

Gift Received: _______________________________
Received From: _______________________________
Date Received: _______________________________
Received Via: _______________________________

Thank You Card Sent: O Yes O No   Date Mailed: [/ /]

Christmas Gift Tracker

Gift Received: _________________________

Received From: _________________________

Date Received: _________________________

Received Via: _________________________

Thank You Card Sent: ◯ Yes ◯ No   Date Mailed: [/   /]

Gift Received: _________________________

Received From: _________________________

Date Received: _________________________

Received Via: _________________________

Thank You Card Sent: ◯ Yes ◯ No   Date Mailed: [/   /]

Gift Received: _________________________

Received From: _________________________

Date Received: _________________________

Received Via: _________________________

Thank You Card Sent: ◯ Yes ◯ No   Date Mailed: [/   /]

Gift Received: _________________________

Received From: _________________________

Date Received: _________________________

Received Via: _________________________

Thank You Card Sent: ◯ Yes ◯ No   Date Mailed: [/   /]

Gift Received: _________________________

Received From: _________________________

Date Received: _________________________

Received Via: _________________________

Thank You Card Sent: ◯ Yes ◯ No   Date Mailed: [/   /]

Christmas Gift Tracker

Gift Received: ________________________
Received From: ________________________
Date Received: ________________________
Received Via: ________________________

Thank You Card Sent: O Yes O No   Date Mailed: [/   /   ]

Gift Received: ________________________
Received From: ________________________
Date Received: ________________________
Received Via: ________________________

Thank You Card Sent: O Yes O No   Date Mailed: [/   /   ]

Gift Received: ________________________
Received From: ________________________
Date Received: ________________________
Received Via: ________________________

Thank You Card Sent: O Yes O No   Date Mailed: [/   /   ]

Gift Received: ________________________
Received From: ________________________
Date Received: ________________________
Received Via: ________________________

Thank You Card Sent: O Yes O No   Date Mailed: [/   /   ]

Gift Received: ________________________
Received From: ________________________
Date Received: ________________________
Received Via: ________________________

Thank You Card Sent: O Yes O No   Date Mailed: [/   /   ]

Christmas Gift Tracker

Gift Received: _______________________

Received From: _______________________

Date Received: _______________________

Received Via: _______________________

Thank You Card Sent: O Yes O No   Date Mailed: [/ /]

Gift Received: _______________________

Received From: _______________________

Date Received: _______________________

Received Via: _______________________

Thank You Card Sent: O Yes O No   Date Mailed: [/ /]

Gift Received: _______________________

Received From: _______________________

Date Received: _______________________

Received Via: _______________________

Thank You Card Sent: O Yes O No   Date Mailed: [/ /]

Gift Received: _______________________

Received From: _______________________

Date Received: _______________________

Received Via: _______________________

Thank You Card Sent: O Yes O No   Date Mailed: [/ /]

Gift Received: _______________________

Received From: _______________________

Date Received: _______________________

Received Via: _______________________

Thank You Card Sent: O Yes O No   Date Mailed: [/ /]

Christmas Gift Tracker

Gift Received:
Received From:
Date Received:
Received Via:

Thank You Card Sent: O Yes O No   Date Mailed: [/   /   ]

Gift Received:
Received From:
Date Received:
Received Via:

Thank You Card Sent: O Yes O No   Date Mailed: [/   /   ]

Gift Received:
Received From:
Date Received:
Received Via:

Thank You Card Sent: O Yes O No   Date Mailed: [/   /   ]

Gift Received:
Received From:
Date Received:
Received Via:

Thank You Card Sent: O Yes O No   Date Mailed: [/   /   ]

Gift Received:
Received From:
Date Received:
Received Via:

Thank You Card Sent: O Yes O No   Date Mailed: [/   /   ]

Christmas Gift Tracker

Gift Received: ___________________________
Received From: ___________________________
Date Received: ___________________________
Received Via: ___________________________

Thank You Card Sent: O Yes O No   Date Mailed: [/ /]

Gift Received: ___________________________
Received From: ___________________________
Date Received: ___________________________
Received Via: ___________________________

Thank You Card Sent: O Yes O No   Date Mailed: [/ /]

Gift Received: ___________________________
Received From: ___________________________
Date Received: ___________________________
Received Via: ___________________________

Thank You Card Sent: O Yes O No   Date Mailed: [/ /]

Gift Received: ___________________________
Received From: ___________________________
Date Received: ___________________________
Received Via: ___________________________

Thank You Card Sent: O Yes O No   Date Mailed: [/ /]

Gift Received: ___________________________
Received From: ___________________________
Date Received: ___________________________
Received Via: ___________________________

Thank You Card Sent: O Yes O No   Date Mailed: [/ /]

Christmas Gift Tracker

Gift Received: ___________________________
Received From: ___________________________
Date Received: ___________________________
Received Via: ___________________________

Thank You Card Sent: O Yes O No   Date Mailed: [/   /   ]

Gift Received: ___________________________
Received From: ___________________________
Date Received: ___________________________
Received Via: ___________________________

Thank You Card Sent: O Yes O No   Date Mailed: [/   /   ]

Gift Received: ___________________________
Received From: ___________________________
Date Received: ___________________________
Received Via: ___________________________

Thank You Card Sent: O Yes O No   Date Mailed: [/   /   ]

Gift Received: ___________________________
Received From: ___________________________
Date Received: ___________________________
Received Via: ___________________________

Thank You Card Sent: O Yes O No   Date Mailed: [/   /   ]

Gift Received: ___________________________
Received From: ___________________________
Date Received: ___________________________
Received Via: ___________________________

Thank You Card Sent: O Yes O No   Date Mailed: [/   /   ]

Christmas Gift Tracker

Gift Received: ______________________________
Received From: ______________________________
Date Received: ______________________________
Received Via: ______________________________

Thank You Card Sent: O Yes O No   Date Mailed: [/ /]

Gift Received: ______________________________
Received From: ______________________________
Date Received: ______________________________
Received Via: ______________________________

Thank You Card Sent: O Yes O No   Date Mailed: [/ /]

Gift Received: ______________________________
Received From: ______________________________
Date Received: ______________________________
Received Via: ______________________________

Thank You Card Sent: O Yes O No   Date Mailed: [/ /]

Gift Received: ______________________________
Received From: ______________________________
Date Received: ______________________________
Received Via: ______________________________

Thank You Card Sent: O Yes O No   Date Mailed: [/ /]

Gift Received: ______________________________
Received From: ______________________________
Date Received: ______________________________
Received Via: ______________________________

Thank You Card Sent: O Yes O No   Date Mailed: [/ /]

Christmas Gift Tracker

Gift Received: _______________________________
Received From: _______________________________
Date Received: _______________________________
Received Via: _______________________________

Thank You Card Sent: O Yes O No   Date Mailed: [/ /]

Gift Received: _______________________________
Received From: _______________________________
Date Received: _______________________________
Received Via: _______________________________

Thank You Card Sent: O Yes O No   Date Mailed: [/ /]

Gift Received: _______________________________
Received From: _______________________________
Date Received: _______________________________
Received Via: _______________________________

Thank You Card Sent: O Yes O No   Date Mailed: [/ /]

Gift Received: _______________________________
Received From: _______________________________
Date Received: _______________________________
Received Via: _______________________________

Thank You Card Sent: O Yes O No   Date Mailed: [/ /]

Gift Received: _______________________________
Received From: _______________________________
Date Received: _______________________________
Received Via: _______________________________

Thank You Card Sent: O Yes O No   Date Mailed: [/ /]

Christmas Gift Tracker

Gift Received: _______________________
Received From: _______________________
Date Received: _______________________
Received Via: _______________________

Thank You Card Sent: O Yes O No   Date Mailed: [/   /   ]

Gift Received: _______________________
Received From: _______________________
Date Received: _______________________
Received Via: _______________________

Thank You Card Sent: O Yes O No   Date Mailed: [/   /   ]

Gift Received: _______________________
Received From: _______________________
Date Received: _______________________
Received Via: _______________________

Thank You Card Sent: O Yes O No   Date Mailed: [/   /   ]

Gift Received: _______________________
Received From: _______________________
Date Received: _______________________
Received Via: _______________________

Thank You Card Sent: O Yes O No   Date Mailed: [/   /   ]

Gift Received: _______________________
Received From: _______________________
Date Received: _______________________
Received Via: _______________________

Thank You Card Sent: O Yes O No   Date Mailed: [/   /   ]

Christmas Gift Tracker

Gift Received: _______________________________
Received From: _______________________________
Date Received: _______________________________
Received Via: _______________________________

Thank You Card Sent: O Yes O No   Date Mailed: [/   /   ]

Gift Received: _______________________________
Received From: _______________________________
Date Received: _______________________________
Received Via: _______________________________

Thank You Card Sent: O Yes O No   Date Mailed: [/   /   ]

Gift Received: _______________________________
Received From: _______________________________
Date Received: _______________________________
Received Via: _______________________________

Thank You Card Sent: O Yes O No   Date Mailed: [/   /   ]

Gift Received: _______________________________
Received From: _______________________________
Date Received: _______________________________
Received Via: _______________________________

Thank You Card Sent: O Yes O No   Date Mailed: [/   /   ]

Gift Received: _______________________________
Received From: _______________________________
Date Received: _______________________________
Received Via: _______________________________

Thank You Card Sent: O Yes O No   Date Mailed: [/   /   ]

Christmas Gift Tracker

Gift Received: ___________________________
Received From: ___________________________
Date Received: ___________________________
Received Via: ___________________________

Thank You Card Sent: O Yes O No   Date Mailed: [/   /   ]

Gift Received: ___________________________
Received From: ___________________________
Date Received: ___________________________
Received Via: ___________________________

Thank You Card Sent: O Yes O No   Date Mailed: [/   /   ]

Gift Received: ___________________________
Received From: ___________________________
Date Received: ___________________________
Received Via: ___________________________

Thank You Card Sent: O Yes O No   Date Mailed: [/   /   ]

Gift Received: ___________________________
Received From: ___________________________
Date Received: ___________________________
Received Via: ___________________________

Thank You Card Sent: O Yes O No   Date Mailed: [/   /   ]

Gift Received: ___________________________
Received From: ___________________________
Date Received: ___________________________
Received Via: ___________________________

Thank You Card Sent: O Yes O No   Date Mailed: [/   /   ]

Christmas Gift Tracker

Gift Received: ______________________________
Received From: ______________________________
Date Received: ______________________________
Received Via: ______________________________

Thank You Card Sent: O Yes O No   Date Mailed: [/   /   ]

Gift Received: ______________________________
Received From: ______________________________
Date Received: ______________________________
Received Via: ______________________________

Thank You Card Sent: O Yes O No   Date Mailed: [/   /   ]

Gift Received: ______________________________
Received From: ______________________________
Date Received: ______________________________
Received Via: ______________________________

Thank You Card Sent: O Yes O No   Date Mailed: [/   /   ]

Gift Received: ______________________________
Received From: ______________________________
Date Received: ______________________________
Received Via: ______________________________

Thank You Card Sent: O Yes O No   Date Mailed: [/   /   ]

Gift Received: ______________________________
Received From: ______________________________
Date Received: ______________________________
Received Via: ______________________________

Thank You Card Sent: O Yes O No   Date Mailed: [/   /   ]

Christmas Gift Tracker

Gift Received: _______________________________
Received From: _______________________________
Date Received: _______________________________
Received Via: _______________________________

Thank You Card Sent: O Yes O No   Date Mailed: [/ /]

Gift Received: _______________________________
Received From: _______________________________
Date Received: _______________________________
Received Via: _______________________________

Thank You Card Sent: O Yes O No   Date Mailed: [/ /]

Gift Received: _______________________________
Received From: _______________________________
Date Received: _______________________________
Received Via: _______________________________

Thank You Card Sent: O Yes O No   Date Mailed: [/ /]

Gift Received: _______________________________
Received From: _______________________________
Date Received: _______________________________
Received Via: _______________________________

Thank You Card Sent: O Yes O No   Date Mailed: [/ /]

Gift Received: _______________________________
Received From: _______________________________
Date Received: _______________________________
Received Via: _______________________________

Thank You Card Sent: O Yes O No   Date Mailed: [/ /]

Christmas Gift Tracker

Gift Received: _______________________________
Received From: _______________________________
Date Received: _______________________________
Received Via: _______________________________

Thank You Card Sent: O Yes O No   Date Mailed: [/   /   ]

Gift Received: _______________________________
Received From: _______________________________
Date Received: _______________________________
Received Via: _______________________________

Thank You Card Sent: O Yes O No   Date Mailed: [/   /   ]

Gift Received: _______________________________
Received From: _______________________________
Date Received: _______________________________
Received Via: _______________________________

Thank You Card Sent: O Yes O No   Date Mailed: [/   /   ]

Gift Received: _______________________________
Received From: _______________________________
Date Received: _______________________________
Received Via: _______________________________

Thank You Card Sent: O Yes O No   Date Mailed: [/   /   ]

Gift Received: _______________________________
Received From: _______________________________
Date Received: _______________________________
Received Via: _______________________________

Thank You Card Sent: O Yes O No   Date Mailed: [/   /   ]

Christmas Gift Tracker

Gift Received: ______________________________
Received From: ______________________________
Date Received: ______________________________
Received Via: ______________________________

Thank You Card Sent: O Yes O No   Date Mailed: [/   /   ]

Gift Received: ______________________________
Received From: ______________________________
Date Received: ______________________________
Received Via: ______________________________

Thank You Card Sent: O Yes O No   Date Mailed: [/   /   ]

Gift Received: ______________________________
Received From: ______________________________
Date Received: ______________________________
Received Via: ______________________________

Thank You Card Sent: O Yes O No   Date Mailed: [/   /   ]

Gift Received: ______________________________
Received From: ______________________________
Date Received: ______________________________
Received Via: ______________________________

Thank You Card Sent: O Yes O No   Date Mailed: [/   /   ]

Gift Received: ______________________________
Received From: ______________________________
Date Received: ______________________________
Received Via: ______________________________

Thank You Card Sent: O Yes O No   Date Mailed: [/   /   ]

Christmas Gift Tracker

Gift Received: ________________________
Received From: ________________________
Date Received: ________________________
Received Via: ________________________

Thank You Card Sent: O Yes O No   Date Mailed: [/ /]

Gift Received: ________________________
Received From: ________________________
Date Received: ________________________
Received Via: ________________________

Thank You Card Sent: O Yes O No   Date Mailed: [/ /]

Gift Received: ________________________
Received From: ________________________
Date Received: ________________________
Received Via: ________________________

Thank You Card Sent: O Yes O No   Date Mailed: [/ /]

Gift Received: ________________________
Received From: ________________________
Date Received: ________________________
Received Via: ________________________

Thank You Card Sent: O Yes O No   Date Mailed: [/ /]

Gift Received: ________________________
Received From: ________________________
Date Received: ________________________
Received Via: ________________________

Thank You Card Sent: O Yes O No   Date Mailed: [/ /]

Christmas Gift Tracker

Gift Received: _______________________________

Received From: _______________________________

Date Received: _______________________________

Received Via: _______________________________

Thank You Card Sent: ○ Yes ○ No   Date Mailed: [__ / __ / __]

Gift Received: _______________________________

Received From: _______________________________

Date Received: _______________________________

Received Via: _______________________________

Thank You Card Sent: ○ Yes ○ No   Date Mailed: [__ / __ / __]

Gift Received: _______________________________

Received From: _______________________________

Date Received: _______________________________

Received Via: _______________________________

Thank You Card Sent: ○ Yes ○ No   Date Mailed: [__ / __ / __]

Gift Received: _______________________________

Received From: _______________________________

Date Received: _______________________________

Received Via: _______________________________

Thank You Card Sent: ○ Yes ○ No   Date Mailed: [__ / __ / __]

Gift Received: _______________________________

Received From: _______________________________

Date Received: _______________________________

Received Via: _______________________________

Thank You Card Sent: ○ Yes ○ No   Date Mailed: [__ / __ / __]

Christmas Gift Tracker

Gift Received: ___________________________
Received From: ___________________________
Date Received: ___________________________
Received Via: ___________________________

Thank You Card Sent: O Yes O No   Date Mailed: [/ /]

Gift Received: ___________________________
Received From: ___________________________
Date Received: ___________________________
Received Via: ___________________________

Thank You Card Sent: O Yes O No   Date Mailed: [/ /]

Gift Received: ___________________________
Received From: ___________________________
Date Received: ___________________________
Received Via: ___________________________

Thank You Card Sent: O Yes O No   Date Mailed: [/ /]

Gift Received: ___________________________
Received From: ___________________________
Date Received: ___________________________
Received Via: ___________________________

Thank You Card Sent: O Yes O No   Date Mailed: [/ /]

Gift Received: ___________________________
Received From: ___________________________
Date Received: ___________________________
Received Via: ___________________________

Thank You Card Sent: O Yes O No   Date Mailed: [/ /]

Christmas Gift Tracker

Gift Received: _______________________

Received From: _______________________

Date Received: _______________________

Received Via: _______________________

Thank You Card Sent: O Yes O No   Date Mailed: [__ / __ / __]

Gift Received: _______________________

Received From: _______________________

Date Received: _______________________

Received Via: _______________________

Thank You Card Sent: O Yes O No   Date Mailed: [__ / __ / __]

Gift Received: _______________________

Received From: _______________________

Date Received: _______________________

Received Via: _______________________

Thank You Card Sent: O Yes O No   Date Mailed: [__ / __ / __]

Gift Received: _______________________

Received From: _______________________

Date Received: _______________________

Received Via: _______________________

Thank You Card Sent: O Yes O No   Date Mailed: [__ / __ / __]

Gift Received: _______________________

Received From: _______________________

Date Received: _______________________

Received Via: _______________________

Thank You Card Sent: O Yes O No   Date Mailed: [__ / __ / __]

Christmas Gift Tracker

Gift Received: _______________________________
Received From: _______________________________
Date Received: _______________________________
Received Via: _______________________________

Thank You Card Sent: O Yes O No   Date Mailed: [/ /]

Gift Received: _______________________________
Received From: _______________________________
Date Received: _______________________________
Received Via: _______________________________

Thank You Card Sent: O Yes O No   Date Mailed: [/ /]

Gift Received: _______________________________
Received From: _______________________________
Date Received: _______________________________
Received Via: _______________________________

Thank You Card Sent: O Yes O No   Date Mailed: [/ /]

Gift Received: _______________________________
Received From: _______________________________
Date Received: _______________________________
Received Via: _______________________________

Thank You Card Sent: O Yes O No   Date Mailed: [/ /]

Gift Received: _______________________________
Received From: _______________________________
Date Received: _______________________________
Received Via: _______________________________

Thank You Card Sent: O Yes O No   Date Mailed: [/ /]

Christmas Gift Tracker

Gift Received: ______________________________
Received From: ______________________________
Date Received: ______________________________
Received Via: ______________________________

Thank You Card Sent: O Yes O No   Date Mailed: [/ /]

Gift Received: ______________________________
Received From: ______________________________
Date Received: ______________________________
Received Via: ______________________________

Thank You Card Sent: O Yes O No   Date Mailed: [/ /]

Gift Received: ______________________________
Received From: ______________________________
Date Received: ______________________________
Received Via: ______________________________

Thank You Card Sent: O Yes O No   Date Mailed: [/ /]

Gift Received: ______________________________
Received From: ______________________________
Date Received: ______________________________
Received Via: ______________________________

Thank You Card Sent: O Yes O No   Date Mailed: [/ /]

Gift Received: ______________________________
Received From: ______________________________
Date Received: ______________________________
Received Via: ______________________________

Thank You Card Sent: O Yes O No   Date Mailed: [/ /]

A Year of Firsts
Part Two
By Rebecca M. Norris

There was the last letter she had ever written to him on her desk. Unopened. He couldn't bring himself to open it. She had known she was dying and didn't tell him. She didn't tell anyone. How could she not tell him something that important? He knew why. She wanted her final days to be full of joy and unchanged routine. That was her way. She never wanted anyone to make a fuss over her. And she certainly didn't want anyone to see her differently or treat her differently. But he was still bitter about her decision. How could he show her just how much he loved her now?

She had complained of being tired on that unforgettable Christmas Day last year. He suggested she go upstairs and take a nap. He would come get her after a while. As she sat at her desk that day, she wrote a letter to each of their three children, and lastly one to her beloved. She died before she finished putting his letter into the envelope. It lay just as he found it, half in the envelope and half out. He would never forget finding her slumped over the desk, a soft smile on her face. *Why was she smiling*, he wondered. He assumed he would never know.

He closed the door to their bedroom, still unable to enter for more than a few moments. As he trudged back down the stairs he paused at the basement door. The Christmas decorations were down there. The kids had to take everything down after she died. He couldn't bring himself to do it. He just sat in his rocking chair like a stone for so long. Guinevere, his oldest daughter, had brought her small children over and took down the tree, the ornaments, everything, and packed it all away in the basement. He just sat in his chair, unmoving. He knew he should help, but why?

Gwen had asked him to decorate this year, for the grandchildren. Maybe next year. His pain was still too raw to celebrate anything this year. He didn't go to anyone's birthday party, he missed his oldest granddaughter's kindergarten graduation, and he didn't attend Gwen's anniversary party. He just couldn't this year, but maybe next year. He kept telling himself that, and it helped him pass the time, but he knew he likely wouldn't next year either.

To Be Continued

Christmas
Recipes

Some More Time
By Scott Norris

You promised to be there
For me, no matter what
And alone I must fair
Through strife, challenge, and rut

That was a great Christmas
The best one I've had yet
I hope to see what was,
Not unending regret.

But now you have gone away,
Both you and my Daddy,
What more is there to say?
Except going on sadly.

It's Christmas time again
Without my family
Will there be a time when,
Joy and love come to me?

One more Christmas with you
Is all that I do need.
My request is all true,
My desire will you heed?

RECIPE

Name: **From:**

Ingredients:

Directions:

Notes:

RECIPE

Name: **From:**

Ingredients:

Directions:

Notes:

RECIPE

Name: **From:**

Ingredients:

Directions:

Notes:

 RECIPE

Name: **From:**

Ingredients:

____

____

____

____

____

____

____

____

____

Directions:

____

____

____

____

____

____

____

____

____

Notes:

____

____

____

____

____

____

____

# RECIPE

Name: From:

Ingredients:

Directions:

Notes:

RECIPE

Name: **From:**

Ingredients:

Directions:

Notes:

Name: **From:**

Ingredients:

____
____
____
____
____
____
____
____

Directions:

____
____
____
____
____
____
____
____
____

Notes:

____
____
____
____
____
____

RECIPE

Name: **From:**

Ingredients:

Directions:

Notes:

RECIPE

Name: **From:**

Ingredients:

Directions:

Notes:

Name: From:

Ingredients:

Directions:

Notes:

RECIPE

Name: **From:**

Ingredients:

Directions:

Notes:

RECIPE

Name: **From:**

Ingredients:

____
____
____
____
____
____
____
____
____

Directions:

____
____
____
____
____
____
____
____
____

Notes:

____
____
____
____
____
____

RECIPE

Name: **From:**

Ingredients:

____
____
____
____
____
____
____
____
____

Directions:

____
____
____
____
____
____
____
____
____

Notes:

____
____
____
____
____
____

RECIPE

Name: **From:**

Ingredients:

Directions:

Notes:

RECIPE

Name: **From:**

Ingredients:

Directions:

Notes:

RECIPE

Name: **From:**

Ingredients:

____
____
____
____
____
____
____
____

Directions:

____
____
____
____
____
____
____
____
____

Notes:

____
____
____
____
____
____

RECIPE

Name: **From:**

Ingredients:

Directions:

Notes:

Name: From:

Ingredients:

Directions:

Notes:

Name: From:

Ingredients:

Directions:

Notes:

RECIPE

Name: **From:**

Ingredients:

Directions:

Notes:

RECIPE

Name: **From:**

Ingredients:

Directions:

Notes:

Name: From:

Ingredients:

Directions:

Notes:

RECIPE

Name: **From:**

Ingredients:

____
____
____
____
____
____
____
____
____

Directions:

____
____
____
____
____
____
____
____
____

Notes:

____
____
____
____
____
____

RECIPE

Name: **From:**

Ingredients:

Directions:

Notes:

Name: **From:**

Ingredients:

Directions:

Notes:

RECIPE

Name: **From:**

Ingredients:

Directions:

Notes:

RECIPE

Name: **From:**

Ingredients:

____
____
____
____
____
____
____
____

Directions:

____
____
____
____
____
____
____
____
____

Notes:

____
____
____
____
____
____

RECIPE

Name: **From:**

Ingredients:

Directions:

Notes:

 RECIPE

Name: **From:**

Ingredients:

Directions:

Notes:

 RECIPE

Name: **From:**

Ingredients:

Directions:

Notes:

A Year of Firsts
Part Three

By Rebecca M. Norris

The phone rang again and he went to answer it. *Now which one is trying to get me to celebrate this year, Gareth or Jennica?* He assumed he would hear from each of his children the closer Christmas came. It was Gareth this time, but he told his son the same thing he told Gwen, maybe next year.

"Dad," Gareth said as he was about to hang up. "Did you ever get around to reading Mom's letter? It took me a long time to open it, too, but I'm glad I did. You really should read it. I think it will help."

"Perhaps, son, perhaps," he said as he hung up. *But I doubt it. Maybe next year.*

Jennica called next, and he said the same thing to his youngest child as he had to the others. Maybe next year. It had become his mantra.

"Daddy," she started. "Please read Momma's letter. She didn't write it in her final moments for it to sit on her desk unopened and you know it." That hurt. He'd never thought of it that way before. Leave it to Jennica to drive the point home like a dagger. She was blunt, but she knew how to get the message across.

"Alright, baby girl," he caved. "I'll read it. I promise I'll go right upstairs and read it as soon as I hang up." He always kept his promises. He never made one he couldn't keep because he seldom ever made one. In fact, he could probably count the times he had made a promise in his life on a four-fingered man's hand and have a finger left over. He would keep his promise to his daughter.

He hung up the phone, gathered his courage, and went back upstairs. His hand trembled on the door, but he had made his little girl a promise. He turned the knob quickly, and rushed into the room holding his breath. He grabbed the letter from the desk and hurried out of the room again before he lost his courage. The tears started to pool in his eyes, so he sat down at the top of the stairs instead of trying to navigate down.

After about ten minutes of letting his emotions run their course, he opened the letter:

To Be Continued

REFRIGERATOR INVENTORY

Purchase Date	Expiration Date	Item	Quantity
Purchase Date	Expiration Date	Item	Quantity

REFRIGERATOR INVENTORY

Purchase Date	Expiration Date	Item	Quantity

REFRIGERATOR INVENTORY

Purchase Date	Expiration Date	Item	Quantity
Purchase Date	Expiration Date	Item	Quantity

REFRIGERATOR INVENTORY

Purchase Date	Expiration Date	Item	Quantity

REFRIGERATOR INVENTORY

Purchase Date	Expiration Date	Item	Quantity
Purchase Date	Expiration Date	Item	Quantity

REFRIGERATOR INVENTORY

Purchase Date	Expiration Date	Item	Quantity
Purchase Date	Expiration Date	Item	Quantity

REFRIGERATOR INVENTORY

Purchase Date	Expiration Date	Item	Quantity
Purchase Date	Expiration Date	Item	Quantity

REFRIGERATOR INVENTORY

Purchase Date	Expiration Date	Item	Quantity

REFRIGERATOR INVENTORY

Purchase Date	Expiration Date	Item	Quantity

REFRIGERATOR INVENTORY

Purchase Date	Expiration Date	Item	Quantity

Purchase Date	Expiration Date	Item	Quantity

REFRIGERATOR INVENTORY

Purchase Date	Expiration Date	Item	Quantity

Purchase Date	Expiration Date	Item	Quantity

REFRIGERATOR INVENTORY

Purchase Date	Expiration Date	Item	Quantity

Purchase Date	Expiration Date	Item	Quantity

REFRIGERATOR INVENTORY

Purchase Date	Expiration Date	Item	Quantity
Purchase Date	Expiration Date	Item	Quantity

REFRIGERATOR INVENTORY

Purchase Date	Expiration Date	Item	Quantity

REFRIGERATOR INVENTORY

Purchase Date	Expiration Date	Item	Quantity
Purchase Date	Expiration Date	Item	Quantity

REFRIGERATOR INVENTORY

Purchase Date	Expiration Date	Item	Quantity
Purchase Date	Expiration Date	Item	Quantity

REFRIGERATOR INVENTORY

Purchase Date	Expiration Date	Item	Quantity

REFRIGERATOR INVENTORY

Purchase Date	Expiration Date	Item	Quantity

REFRIGERATOR INVENTORY

Purchase Date	Expiration Date	Item	Quantity
Purchase Date	Expiration Date	Item	Quantity

REFRIGERATOR INVENTORY

Purchase Date	Expiration Date	Item	Quantity

A Year of Firsts
Part Four
By Rebecca M. Norris

To My Cherished One,

I know you must be feeling some very strong emotions as you read this, and I know you well enough to know one of those emotions is bitterness. How could I have kept my illness a secret from you, my very best friend? Please try to understand things from my perspective.

I knew my final days in this body would pass quickly. I knew I would be leaving everyone confused and shocked. I have written letters to Gwen, Jennica, and Gareth explaining why their mother kept this secret, but writing to you is proving to be far more difficult.

There are so many things I want to tell you, so many dreams we shared that will never be. Remember how we said we would sit out on the front porch when you turned 90 and sip our favorite tea as we watched the sunset? I still want you to do that, but I know you probably won't. It wouldn't be the same dream without me there, would it?

I would say time heals all wounds, but it doesn't. Time only takes the edge off, the pain remains. I am pained to know that I must leave you soon. Very soon, I think. I hope I make it through Christmas Day, but something tells me I won't be going back downstairs today. Please remember why we celebrate Christmas Day, my love. Don't let my passing taint the wonder and beauty of this day!

Remember that Christmas isn't about gifts or decorations or even about that apple pie I keep saying I'll make one of these years. It is about a little baby born long, long ago. It is about the God of Heaven Who loved us so much that He became one of us to understand us and save us. We celebrate this miraculous gift on Christmas Day. Don't ever forget that. No one person on Earth should ever replace the One born on Christmas Day, not even me.

I know it will be hard for you after I'm gone. I don't have any easy answers for you. Just know that I am at peace, I am happy, and I am waiting patiently for the time when you can come join me in Heaven with our Savior. Find your joy again, my love. Remember the why, and never stop celebrating the One that gave us a lifetime together. A life I have loved from the first moment! You have made my life so full of love and joy, there's not one thing I would change. Not one!

Oh, my cherished husband. It is time for me to go now. I love you, and I will wait for the day we meet again. Live your life, my love! Find your joy again! That is what you always tell me, isn't it? One final thought that I hope you carry with you each day. I am always and forever in your heart. No one can ever take that away from you.

Goodbye for a little while,
Your Beloved

The Be Continued

Let's Go See The Christmas Lights!
By Scott Norris

Let's go see the Christmas lights!
Shining, twinkling these great nights,
They make pretty Christmas sights.

Let's go see the lights displays!
A glowing show on these great days,
Home sized décor will amaze!

Let's go see the lights, we will?
In our car, I will sit still!
Don't speak of their power bill!

Let's go see the Christmas lights!
Red, Green, White, bulbs bring delights!
Christmas cheer will hit new heights!

So let's go-oo, see those lights!

Meal
Planner

DECEMBER 01

Breakfast

Lunch

Dinner

Dessert

DECEMBER 02

Breakfast

Lunch

Dinner

Dessert

DECEMBER 03

Breakfast

Lunch

Dinner

Dessert

DECEMBER 04

Breakfast

Lunch

Dinner

Dessert

DECEMBER 05

Breakfast

Lunch

Dinner

Dessert

DECEMBER 06

Breakfast

Lunch

Dinner

Dessert

DECEMBER 07

Breakfast

Lunch

Dinner

Dessert

DECEMBER 08

Breakfast

Lunch

Dinner

Dessert

DECEMBER 09

Breakfast

Lunch

Dinner

Dessert

DECEMBER 10

Breakfast

Lunch

Dinner

Dessert

DECEMBER 11

Breakfast

Lunch

Dinner

Dessert

DECEMBER 12

Breakfast

Lunch

Dinner

Dessert

DECEMBER 13

Breakfast

Lunch

Dinner

Dessert

DECEMBER 14

Breakfast

Lunch

Dinner

Dessert

DECEMBER 15

Breakfast

Lunch

Dinner

Dessert

DECEMBER 16

Breakfast

Lunch

Dinner

Dessert

DECEMBER 17

Breakfast

Lunch

Dinner

Dessert

DECEMBER 18

Breakfast

Lunch

Dinner

Dessert

DECEMBER 19

Breakfast

Lunch

Dinner

Dessert

DECEMBER 20

Breakfast

Lunch

Dinner

Dessert

DECEMBER 21

Breakfast

Lunch

Dinner

Dessert

DECEMBER 22

Breakfast

Lunch

Dinner

Dessert

DECEMBER 23

Breakfast

Lunch

Dinner

Dessert

DECEMBER 24

Breakfast

Lunch

Dinner

Dessert

DECEMBER 25

Breakfast

Lunch

Dinner

Dessert

DECEMBER 26

Breakfast

Lunch

Dinner

Dessert

DECEMBER 27

Breakfast

Lunch

Dinner

Dessert

DECEMBER 28

Breakfast

Lunch

Dinner

Dessert

DECEMBER 29

Breakfast

Lunch

Dinner

Dessert

DECEMBER 30

Breakfast

Lunch

Dinner

Dessert

DECEMBER 31

Breakfast

Lunch

Dinner

Dessert

A Year of Firsts
Part Five
By Rebecca M. Norris

Oh, my beautiful bride," he sobbed as he held the letter close to his heart. She did understand how he would feel. She knew how hard the first year without her would be, and she tried to help him.

He remembered telling her that he would always be in her heart. At the time, he was so sure he would be the first to die. He never imagined having to live without her, but that didn't mean the statement was any less true. She was in his heart and always would be.

He looked around the old house with new eyes. He tried to see things the way she did as she went upstairs for that last time. He couldn't do it.

"Something's missing," he said aloud. He went down to the basement and brought up all of the Christmas decorations. He busily set about decorating the house for the most wonderful time of the year. He hadn't realized it until he set the star on top of the tree, but he was singing her favorite Christmas song the entire time. She really was in his heart. This was how he could show her how much he loved her! And he would do so every year that he was able.

He hurried out to the stores and bought gifts for everyone, and then he called the kids to ask them to come over on Christmas Eve and spend the night. He bought the Christmas goose they always had, although it had cost him a fortune this late in the season. He didn't mind, his bride always had a goose and he wasn't about to change that now.

Everything was ready. The table was set, the kids would soon arrive, the house and yard were decorated, and the Christmas music was softly playing in the background. He took the apple pie out of the oven, his new tradition after his Year of Firsts, and grabbed his cup of tea.

Sitting out on the front porch watching the sunset he whispered softly in the growing dusk, a soft smile on his lips.

"Merry Christmas, my beloved. I found my joy again!"

The End

<u>Poems & Story from the 1st Edition</u>

<u>Christmas Come Soon</u>
By Scott Norris

Christmas will be here
Before a long last
With hope, joy, and cheer
From the future and past

With a song in heart
Voices let joy flow
Grins and laughs will start
As carolers go

Tree lights will soon shine
Each home will soon glow
All a hopeful shrine
The best time to know

Families together
To make merry and see
Despite bad weather,
This is true beauty

Christmas please soon come
Let each life see worth
In celebration
Of the Savior's birth.

<u>Time to Trim the Tree</u>
By Scott Norris

Time to trim the tree!
Get the lights to shine
Bring the family
Ornaments divine!

Christmas carols play
Cheer serenades me
As we talk all day
While trimming the tree!

A proud angel tops
Evergreen beauty
While the tinsel pops
Our homes majesty

'Til end of the year
Great tree will stand tall
With hopes we hold dear
No, he will not fall

So come and join me
Come close and stand near
Time to trim the tree,
Yes that time is here!

Birth of Christ
By Scott Norris

Our Lord came to Earth
Born of God, not man
The noblest birth
Mankind's hopeful plan

A baby boy was He
From Heaven above
God became a man
To show the world love

We celebrate life
On this Christmas Day
His great end to strife
A hopeful display

He endured the cross
Good news for all
To avoid the loss
From grace we did fall

Forgiveness is here
For all to receive
The birth we hold dear
Came on Christmas Eve

Here's to the New Year!
By Scott Norris

Here's to the New Year!
Time of hope and love
For all we hold dear,
And care from above

May peace and joy reign
From midwinter to yule
Only worthwhile gain
For those lead and rule

May time with friends grow
And loved ones stay near
As together we go
About this new year

Dreams and hopes alive
From unity's strength
As all will soon strive
The curious length

Here's to the new year
With blessings and care,
To those we hold dear
There's no greater fare.

A Christmas Wish

By Rebecca M. Norris

Talitha woke early in the bitter cold of the morning. She wrapped her tattered shawl around her shoulders as she waited for the matron to collect her. Today was a very important day. She boarded the orphan train today. Part of her was excited that she was boarding the train this time. She wasn't allowed to go on the last train because she had broken her wrist, but she was all better now. Well, almost. She couldn't move it but so far, and she couldn't hold anything with that hand, and sometimes it smarted when it rained, but other than that she was all better. There was another part of her, though, that was frightened at the thought of leaving the only home she had ever known. And what if no one wanted her?

Her father was killed by a widow-maker two years ago, and her mother – who was in the family way at the time – was taken away from her, too, in an early childbirth. They say the strain and grief of losing her husband caused her time to come too soon. She just didn't have the strength to fight. Talitha wondered why her momma didn't want to fight to stay with her. Why didn't she at least try? At just seven years old, Talitha had the weight of the world on her tiny shoulders. In one month she went from a happy-go-lucky five year old, eagerly awaiting the new baby, to an orphan who hadn't spoken a word since her momma looked at her as she breathed her last and said, "I'm sorry, baby. I just can't."

She stared out of the window at a little family walking below. She was the same age as the little girl down there, and there was a small boy being held in his father's arms. They looked so happy. Together. Talitha sighed, and pulled her shawl closer as a tear trickled down her cheek. Perhaps she would have a family of her own come Christmas.

"Come along, Talitha," the matron said as she entered the room. "It's time to go to the train station. Be prompt!"

Talitha gathered her small bag – there was only one item inside, a wooden bear her papa had made for her. He had given it to her the day he died. She knew that if she had just held him a little tighter that day, he wouldn't have wanted to go the long way to the mercantile in the snow. Then the branch wouldn't have fallen on him and the wagon. If she had just held him tighter, if she had just been good enough for her momma to *want* to stay with her, if only... she didn't have time for regrets. Maybe she could start over in a new town, right? Where no one knew her and no one really cared about her past.

The train passed town after town, city after city, from West Virginia to the final stop in Missouri. Each time they came to one of the towns Talitha would wait patiently hoping someone would choose to adopt her. She waited, and waited, and waited. Finally, they arrived at the station in Kansas City, the last stop. And she was the last child on the orphan train on Christmas Day.

"Come along, Talitha, be prompt!" The matron clearly didn't want to do this either. She wasn't a cold-hearted woman, the opposite in fact. She hated coming to the final stop with even one child left unwanted. Her heart broke for little Talitha, but she couldn't break down in front of her either.

Talitha followed the matron. It was cold, but not as cold as West Virginia. Dryer, too. Talitha wondered how close she was to the big water her papa told her about.

"Hello there, Matron Bromwell," a gentleman said and glanced down at Talitha. "Only one for us this time? Well, that's fine! Fine! We're all ready inside. Folks say it's going to snow today. Could be any time now. We have folks that drove in all the way from Dodge City to see the orphan..."

Talitha stopped paying attention and looked at the sky. Snow? Momma said that if Talitha could catch the first snowflake on her nose then she would be granted one wish. Just one wish. Talitha knew exactly what she would wish for, too. Someone to love her again. Arms to hold her and rock her to sleep with a wondrous bedtime story. A smile to greet her when she woke. A laugh so warm that it could melt all the ice in the world. That was her wish. But, she was the last child on the train. The one that always came back to the orphanage because no one wanted them. She couldn't bear the thought.

Please, oh please let me catch just one snowflake, she prayed. Suddenly, as she was about to go inside the meeting hall, it snowed. She ran back outside to find the first one. *There!* She ran and knelt down just as the snowflake hit her nose. She closed her eyes and wished with all that she was.

"Come along now, Talitha, be prompt!" The matron smiled as she watched Talitha, but she also had people waiting to see this little girl. Talitha hurried to catch up.

As soon as the gentleman announced Matron Bromwell and Talitha stood up next to her, dozens of people left. The matron was flustered, but continued her speech nonetheless. By the time the matron was finished everyone had left. Talitha wiped away a tear and pulled her shawl closer.

"Come along now, Talitha," Matron Bromwell said. "We mustn't let…" she burst into tears.

"Oh, Talitha, sweetheart, I'm so sorry." She pulled Talitha in for a tight hug. Talitha simply nodded. Her Christmas wish did not come true.

Matron Bromwell and Talitha gathered their things and walked back to the train station. There were only a few minutes left before their train would leave. There would be another orphan train next year, Talitha knew, but she wouldn't be on it. She would stay and work in the kitchens of the orphanage. She just couldn't go through this again. It hurt too much. No one wanted *her.*

"Wait! Oh, please wait!" A young woman was running towards them. Just behind her was a young man, hobbling along with a cane. Matron Bromwell stopped and turned towards them.

"Yes," she said. "May I help you?"

"Are you Matron Bromwell? With the orphan train?" The young man had a wonderful voice, Talitha thought, the kind that could tell a simply perfect bedtime story. After the matron nodded the man continued.

"We were late arriving, you see," he gestured towards his leg, "and we heard there was a little girl that wasn't adopted. Would that be you, my dear?" Talitha simply nodded once.

The woman looked a little concerned at Talitha's disrespectful response until the matron spoke softly to her.

"She hasn't spoken a word since her parents died. She has a good heart, but we simply can't get her to speak."

"Ah," the woman said gently. She knelt down in the gathering snow and held out her hand. "My name is Gertie Winthrop. This is my husband, Jeffrey. It's quite alright if you don't want to speak just yet, I understand. May I shake your hand instead?"

Talitha held out her crippled hand, but quickly hid it beneath her shawl.

"Talitha broke her wrist, you see, and it hasn't quite healed proper yet," the matron spoke up.

The couple looked at each other and Talitha turned to board the train. The whistle blew, there wasn't much time. She knew how this would end. No one wanted a crippled mute sever-year-old girl around.

"Talitha?" The man gently held her shoulder. Talitha tried to hide the tears in her eyes. Tried, but failed. The man used his own finger to lift a tear from her face as he knelt awkwardly next to his wife in the piling snow.

"I hope that is the last time you will shed sad tears, sweet girl. You see, I can't use my leg anymore, just like you can't use your hand. That's why I became a doctor. To help people just like you. And I lost my parents to a blizzard when I was a child, too. In fact, I was on an orphan train just like you, as was Gertie. It's how we met. We have a very special love for orphans, and we have been praying for a little girl just like you. A little girl that no one else wanted because she was *saved* just for *us*. Would you like to come and live with us in Dodge City? It's quite a trip back, but it would give us lots of time to tell you our story."

"He's a wonderful storyteller, Talitha," Gertie said as she gave her the best hug she'd had in two years. "I have always enjoyed the fantastical places he imagines. And I know he would love to tell you bedtime stories!" She laughed. It was a laugh so warm that it could melt ice. Just like her Christmas wish!

"Well, Talitha," Matron Bromwell smiled down at her. "You don't have to go with them if you don't want to, but something tells me they are the perfect family for you. Would you like to be adopted by them?"

She looked into their eyes and saw a genuine love for her even though they just met her. *Could this be true*, she thought. *Could they really want someone like me when no one else does?* The answer she received to her silent question confirmed what she had already decided.

"Yes!" Talitha cried and fell into her new momma's arms. Her new papa wrapped his arms around them both and she felt tears fall from his cheeks onto her forehead. They truly loved her. Her wish had come true, and on Christmas Day! This was the best present ever!

About the Authors:

Scott Norris

Scott Norris is a Christian fantasy and comedy author who lives in Kansas City with his wife and children. He holds a master's degree in cross-cultural ministry and has travelled the world. When he is not drinking copious amounts of coffee or planning for Christmas, he is telling jokes at his TV.

And thank you reading this, as not everyone has thought to do so.

Visit me at scott-norris.com or scottnorriswrites.medium.com

Rebecca M. Norris

Rebecca M. Norris is a lover of all things science fiction and fantasy. She even had a Lord of the Rings themed wedding! She currently resides in Kansas City with her husband, who is a fellow author, and their children; happily enjoying the chaos that comes from being a mommy. Mostly, Rebecca M. Norris is just your average woman who loves life and the people she shares it with, including you, her readers!

Visit her at rebeccanorrisbooks.com!

<u>By Scott Norris</u>

The Chronicles of Solatia
Book One: Marno's Shield

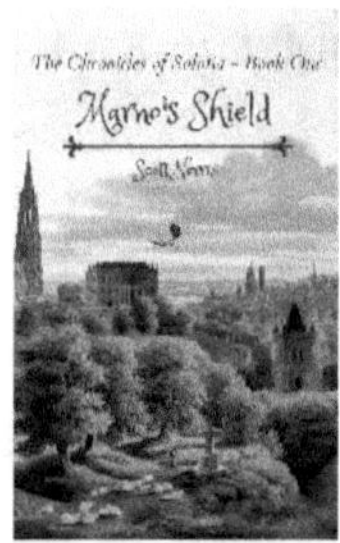

In the country of Syren, young boys are becoming men in the time-honored tradition of the Age of Ascension Ceremony. Upon the conclusion of the ceremony, the King of Syren and the King of Maif sign a lasting treaty of peace. Marno, who just passed his Ascension, believes his future is bright.

Then a betrayal of epic proportions throws his world into chaos. Marno and his best friend, Tigrand, must sacrifice everything in a war they are ill prepared for… or lose it all forever.

Book Two Coming 2023!!!

The Best of the Salty Cee
Vol. 2: Christian News Satire

by John Spencer, Nick Angelis, **Scott Norris**

The Salty Cee is an online Christian News Satire website that doesn't take itself too seriously. This second volume contains another batch of more than 40 of their best-loved articles that poke fun at Christian culture and celebrities.

By Rebecca M. Norris

The Legendary Adventures of Captain Grant Mason
Book One: Captain Grant Mason vs The Black Talons

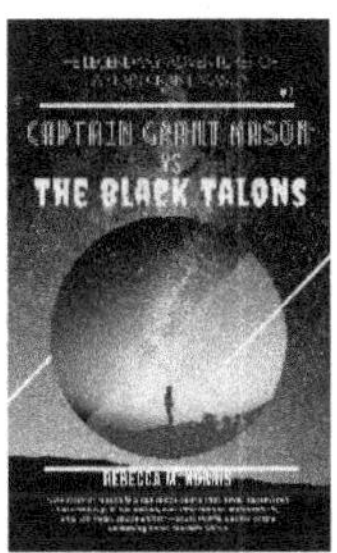

Grant Mason and his crew must fight their way through the Black Market Conglomerate to locate the Black Talons, the weapons dealers and mercenaries of the galaxy. Their assignment: acquire magnatronic particle dispersers from the Talons for use in the war against K'Lon. Simple right? Nothing is ever simple for Grant Mason...

Join Grant and his unique crew as they embark on an epic mission filled with intense danger, certain death, laughable mishaps, stunning surprises, and of course... legendary adventure!

The Halls of Carson High
Book One: Riverside Redemption

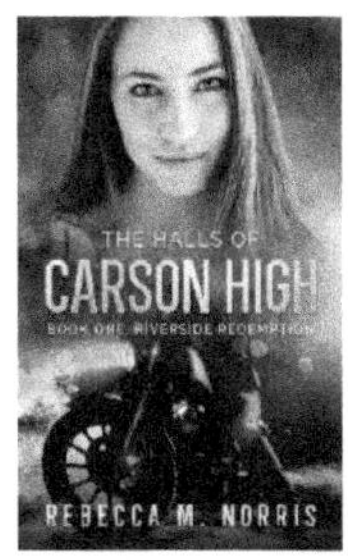

Julianne Hathaway was named "Most Considerate" by her classmates. She was an excellent student who always took time for others. Until she met Bruce Weber, that is...

Bruce Weber was a tough guy. He got along just fine on his own. He didn't care who he hurt as long as he got his way. He had few friends and the whole town hated him. But when Julie Hathaway walked into his life everything changed...

Their two worlds collide as Julie discovers a tragic secret that Bruce works desperately to hide. He knows what will happen if the truth is revealed, but Julie is determined to help him, no matter the cost.

Redemption is just around the corner for Bruce, if Julie can only reach him in time...

This exciting new series for young adults will take you on an adventure filled with mystery, danger, heartache and profound joy as our main characters tackle difficult situations while learning more about themselves and God.

Book Two Coming 2023!

Check out our line of journals at:

www.rebeccanorrisbooks.com/shop

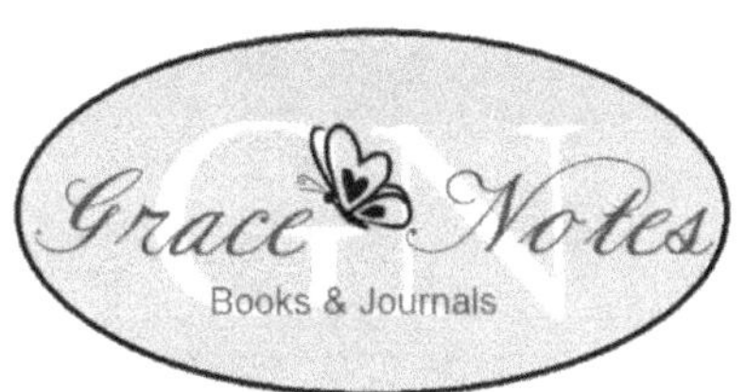

Over 200 journals to choose from!

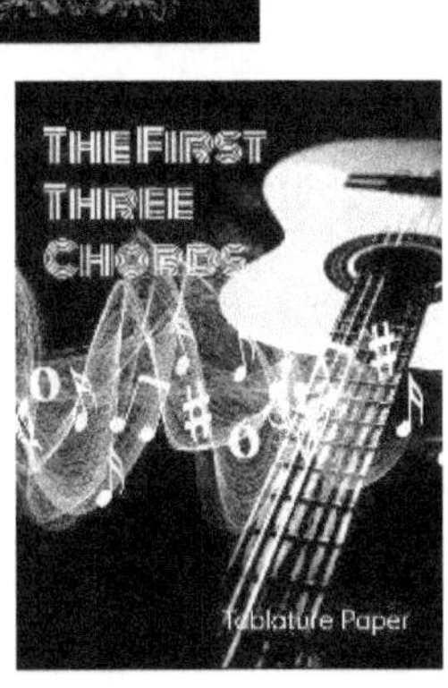

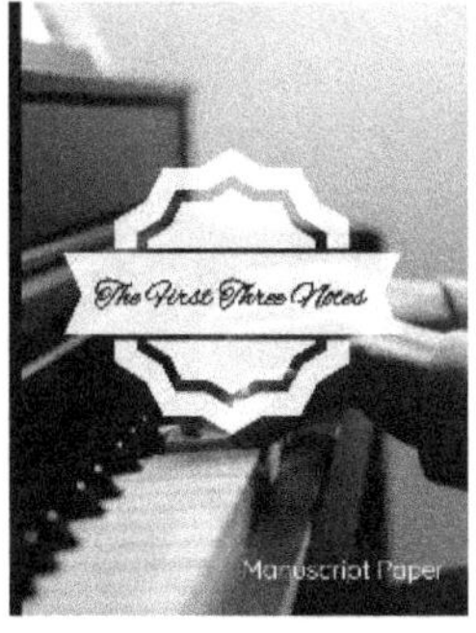

Order yours today!

Made in the U.S.A.

Duskraven Entertainment, LLC

P.O. Box 3795
Olathe, KS 66063

www.ingramcontent.com/pod-product-compliance
Lightning Source LLC
Chambersburg PA
CBHW071230300726
48975CB00002B/354